The Devil
Doll

GHOST HUNTERS SOCIETY

Book Two

Adria Waters

Published by: H2O Press

ISBN-13: 978-0-9973424-7-5
ISBN-10: 0-9973424-7-1

Cover by Covered Creatively

For Brynn,
Love you always.

CHAPTER 1

"Schlafe, mein Kindlein, schlaf ein.
Am Himmel strahlen die Sternelein.
Mache schnell die Aeuglein zu,
So findest du deine Ruh."

The little girl swept a wisp of blonde hair out of her face and rocked her doll in its cradle as she sang in a soft voice. Sunlight skittered through the kitchen windows and onto the worn linoleum, sending splashes of buttery light onto the fleece blanket she was sitting on while she played with her dolls.

"Hannah?"

The little girl looked up as her mother knelt down beside her. "Yes, Mommy?"

"What is that song you're singing?"

The little girl shrugged and kept rocking her doll.

Kristen stood up and wiped her hands on the towel. Brushing her hair out of her eyes, she stared down at her daughter quizzically. "Maybe she learned it at daycare," she mumbled and shook her head. She ruffled Hannah's hair as she turned to look at the boxes of dishes waiting to be unpacked in the kitchen. She sighed. The moving company had broken several things already and she was taking photos of the damage, as she washed the remaining dishes, making sure to rinse off any shards of glass. It was tedious work, which afforded her lots of time to think about why she hated this kitchen, this house...this whole town so much.

When Dalton moved them out here to the middle of nowhere, she thought she'd do just fine. She'd even found Culvers Grove charming at first, covered as it was in a layer of freshly fallen snow with twinkling Christmas lights on all of the houses. They found a whitewashed two-story house on a gravel road near the outskirts of the tiny town. It had black shutters and a tire swing hanging from the tree in the front yard. The lights from the nearest neighbor could be seen at night and Kristen thought, for the moment at least, that she might learn to like the quiet and solitude of the country after living in the hustle and bustle of the city so long. Now, only a few weeks later, the location had lost its charm in her eyes. The town was much too small for her taste.

She hailed from Chicago and met Dalton during her last year of college. He was handsome and smart and a hopeless wanderlust, which is why his career as a Field Service Engineer suited him so well. In the short ten years they'd been married, they moved from Chicago to Miami to Dubai before he was assigned to work on a huge project in St. Joseph, Missouri. They decided to settle in Dalton's hometown so Kristen could be close to his aging mother and help out. He commuted and left early in the morning, before the sun was even awake, sometimes staying overnight in the city an hour and a half away.

She sighed again. His absence left her to do all of the unpacking, and judging by the state she found the first few boxes in that she unpacked, it was going to be quite a job. She rolled her eyes as she dipped a plate in the hot dishwater. At least she had Hannah to keep her company. Kristen smiled. Maybe they'd put up the tree if she got to the boxes in the living room later. Christmas was only a few weeks away and Hannah was so excited about the fireplace. This was the first house she'd ever lived in with one and she was already making plans to sleep on the couch so she could catch Santa Claus in the act.

The light in the kitchen dimmed as a cloud passed between the earth and the sun. The wind picked up outside and Kristen watched a patch of ornamental grass bend and whip back and forth, the sandpaper sound carrying across the yard to her ears. An icy breeze blew in through the screen in the window above the sink, caressing Kristen's cheek with the promise of snow. She wasn't quite used to Missouri weather yet and was surprised at its bipolar nature. Last night they went to bed with extra covers, and today, all the snow was melting under the sun's rays. The windows were open all morning, the fresh air welcome in the musty old house.

"Come on, kiddo. Let's get the windows upstairs closed before it rains, then we'll eat some lunch." She pulled the window down, the old wood creaking in protest against the frame. Twisting the lock on the top of the window, Kristen turned, tossing the towel on the counter.

Suddenly, she noticed how quiet the kitchen was. Kristen cocked her head to the side. "Hannah?"

Hannah had been sitting in the square of sunlight all morning, tending to her dolls and singing her newest song. Kristen sighed and skirted around the table piled high with boxes. "Honey, did you hear me?" The words faded in her mouth as she looked at the blanket. Hannah wasn't in the kitchen anymore. Her favorite doll lay discarded face down on the floor, its hair a tangled halo around its head, and its legs turned in angles that made them appear broken. Kristen leaned down and picked up the doll, smoothing its hair and dress absently as she peered into the small dining room. "Hannah?"

"...*Mache schnell die Aeuglein zu, So findest du deine Ruh...*"

Frigid air blew in through the screen door, whipping Hannah's small voice through the kitchen, making it hard to tell where it was coming from. Gooseflesh rose on Kristen's arms and she pushed the back door closed, locking it against the winter. She placed the doll on the table and walked through the pocket doors to the living room. She leaned over the couch and then checked the front door. Locked. At least Hannah was still in the house. The thought should have comforted her, but this old house was filled with dozens of nooks and crannies and she hadn't had time to clean them all and make sure they were safe for her little girl. "Come on, Hannah! Mommy doesn't have time for this this morning!" Kristen pulled open the small angled door under the stairs and yanked the chain to turn on the lone lightbulb. Nothing but cobwebs and mouse droppings. She would have to clean that out later. Kristen headed upstairs, the treads creaking under her socked feet.

"...*Mache schnell die Aeuglein zu, So findest du deine Ruh...*"

Kristen hesitated, her foot poised above the last step. The singing sounded like it was coming from downstairs, but sound didn't travel like it did in an apartment or a newer, more open floorplan. Kristen shook her head and climbed the last stair. She stopped outside Hannah's door, her hand on the doorknob.

"...*Mache schnell die Aeuglein zu, So findest du deine Ruh...*"

"Hannah?" Kristen turned the doorknob and pushed the door open. Her eyes took a moment to adjust to the darkness of the room. She tried to flip on the light. There was a small fizzing sound as she clicked the switch up and down and then the light flared above her, and with a pop, went out entirely. "Hannah? Are you hiding, sweetie?" She walked around the room slowly, checking all of the places a four-year-old could hide. The latch on the closet door rattled and Kristen froze, relief washing over her and a smile spreading across her face. "There you are, you little imp," she whispered.

When they moved in, Hannah claimed the closet as her favorite spot in her new bedroom. Not only did it have a bar she could reach for all of her clothes and space along the bottom for her shoes, but it was what was behind the closet that Hannah really fell in love with. In the farthest corner of the closet near the stairs on the other side of the wall, there was a small opening, large enough for a child to crawl through. It led to a hidden room behind the closet. The room was cedar lined with a slanted ceiling. It was big enough for a lamp, pillow, and a blanket. Hannah had been stowing books in there since moving in and the box that held them during the move was nearly empty at this point.

Kristen got down on her hands and knees and moved the clothes to the side. A shaft of light spilled out from the secret room into the closet. She crawled forward until her head was almost even with the opening.

She smiled and lunged at the opening, yelling, "Gotcha!"

Hannah's face whipped around, her eyes wide. Then the lamp turned off, plunging the entire little room into darkness.

"Hannah, turn that back on!" Kristen fumbled in her jeans pocket, pulling her phone out and swiping her finger across the screen. The closet was bathed in the blue light and some of Hannah's sequined shirts sparkled. Kristen pushed the phone into the small space and shined it around.

Other than the dark lamp and the pile of books, the space was completely empty. "Hannah, where did you go?" Kristen swiped again at her phone and pulled up the flashlight app, spreading the bright LED light into the space.

There was no one.

"Hannah?" Kristen squeaked out. She was *sure* she saw Hannah. Didn't she? Kristen shook her head, trying to clear it. Maybe she only saw what she'd wanted to see. Dalton told her all the time that she needed to be more practical, less prone to imagination. She put her phone back in her pocket, trying to quell the panic that was beginning to set in as she backed out of the closet. Kristen stood up. "Hannah?" she called to the empty room. She whipped open the blinds and allowed the weak winter sun to illuminate the bedroom. White hot tendrils of panic were beginning to wind their way through her arms and legs, and she took a deep breath.

"Calm down. She's here somewhere. She didn't just disappear." Another deep breath. This time, she spoke loudly, "Hannah, I need you to come out! We have to get lunch ready and then we can put up the Christmas tree for Santa!" Ears straining to hear any movement at all, any response, muscles taut, Kristen waited. Nothing.

Hannah wasn't here. Kristen backed out of the room and closed the door behind her. She checked the upstairs bathroom, brushing the curtain back with a metallic rattle of rings on the rod. Nothing. Then she checked the bedroom that she shared with Dalton, getting down on her knees to look under the bed. Nothing.

Hannah wasn't upstairs anywhere. Kristen stood at the top of the stairs. Was she sure that Hannah hadn't wandered into the back yard? She replayed the morning as she looked back down the hallway, her heart hammering in her chest. If Hannah got outside, she might go into the road, or worse, into the forest at the back of the property.

Stomach twisting in painful knots, Kristen sprinted down the stairs. She ran through the kitchen, and had barely placed her hand on the doorknob when she heard a small voice:

"...*Mache schnell die Aeuglein zu, So findest du deine Ruh...*"

Tears stung the backs of her eyes. "Hannah! Come out!" She followed the last notes of the song through the kitchen to the pantry. Taking a deep breath, she reached up and pulled the chain to turn on the light. The lightbulb swung with her yank, distorting the cans lining the shelves in its moving arc of light. The basement door near the back of the pantry stood partially open, the concrete stairs chipped and uneven leading down into the darkness.

Kristen opened the door another inch or two, the hinges squeaking as she did so. The light in the pantry only reached as far as the third step and blackness spread below. Kristen flipped the switch by the door and somehow wasn't surprised that the light didn't work. She pulled up the flashlight on her phone again and started down the stairs. When she reached the bottom, the silence and darkness pressed in on her.

"Hannah?" Her voice sounded weak even to her own ears and she crept forward, stepping as far as the light from her phone allowed. She'd only been down here once when they looked at the house with the real estate agent, and remembered the basement being split into several rooms, but for the life of her, she couldn't seem to remember the layout. Bathed in the small circle of light from her phone, she walked along the left wall from the stairs. Her hand swept along the concrete wall, cold and rough on her palm. She thought there was a doorway along this wall, but couldn't be sure.

Kristen cried out as her hand met with open space and she almost lost her balance. A small space lined with wooden shelves was along here and the narrow room spread out into another room. Kristen followed the wall into the second room. Down here, the basement had an earthy smell. The floors turned from concrete to dirt and her socks were soon cold and damp against her feet. She shivered and continued to move through room to room.

"Hannah!" Kristen called out. "Hannah, please come to Mommy!"

A small voice singing was her answer,

"...Mache schnell die Aeuglein zu, So findest du deine Ruh..."

It built, amplifying around her and echoing off the walls, leaving her nowhere to escape as the singing battered her. Tears escaped from Kristen's eyes, splashing onto her cheeks. She pressed her back against the wall and let the sobs wrack her body as the song nearly shattered her eardrums.

Then, as suddenly as it started, it stopped. The ringing in her ears whined as she pulled out her phone, dialing Dalton's number as she shivered against the wall.

He answered with a curt, "Hello."

"Dalton, I can't find Hannah! Something really strange is going on! I hear her singing in the basement, but I can't find her!"

"Honey, you know I'm in a meeting. What do you mean you can't find her?"

Kristen was practically screaming into the phone at this point. "I can't find her! She was right here in the kitchen with me and then she was gone! I can't find her!"

Kristen froze as a sound wound its way to her ears. "Mommy?"

The light in the basement blazed to life and Kristen was able to get her bearings. She heard singing. This time, it was coming from the farthest corner of the basement. It was soft and the same line over and over again, *"...Mache schnell die Aeuglein zu, So findest du deine Ruh..."*

Kristen raced through the labyrinth of rooms and skidded to a stop at the back room. There, in the corner, Hannah knelt, hunched over, her back to Kristen.

Kristen let the hand holding the phone fall to her side. "Hannah? Honey?" She took a few steps forward. "Hannah?"

When she got a little closer, she could hear a rasping sound coming from the corner. Hannah continued to sing softly, her attention on the floor in the corner. Kristen crept around and looked down.

Hannah was digging at the dirt floor, her fingernails bloody as she raked them through the hard earth.

"Hannah!" Kristen bent down and scooped the little girl off the floor, cradling her against her chest. Tears ran down her face as she hugged her daughter to her.

"Hi, Mommy." Hannah's big blue eyes turned to her mother and she smiled. "I'm hungry. Can we eat lunch?"

"Of course, we can." Kristen hugged Hannah against her again. "You scared Mommy when I couldn't find you!"

"Kristen, you there?" Dalton's voice came through the phone speaker, tinny and far away.

Kristen brought the phone to her ear. "I found her."

"Oh, good. Listen, I have to get back to my meeting. I'll see you guys around seven tonight. Love you."

"Love you, Daddy!" Hannah called out toward the phone.

"Love you, too, Bug."

"Bye," Kristen mumbled before hitting the button to end the call. "Let's get you cleaned up and then we'll eat, okay?" She struggled to calm her breathing as she held her little girl in a tight embrace.

As they walked away, Hannah leaned her chin on her mother's shoulder. She smiled at her new friend and reached out a pudgy hand to wave goodbye as her mother carried her through the basement and up the stairs.

One painted glass eye stared up from the dirt, following the little girl as she was carried away.

CHAPTER 2

Dad rolled a candy in his mouth and it clicked against his teeth. It was the only sound in the otherwise silent cab of the pickup truck. I leaned against the door, staring out at the skeletal limbs of the trees as we drove along the highway to the hospital. I glanced in the side mirror and saw Andy and Tristan following behind in Andy's truck.

"You all right?" Dad's voice was gruff and he cleared his throat. "I mean about going to see her."

I nodded but didn't turn my head. I hadn't seen him much in the last couple of days. He'd spent Christmas Eve and Christmas Day there, coming home only to shower, grab files from his office, and try to talk me into going to the hospital to see Evie. This afternoon, I finally relented.

I don't need to go to the hospital. It's not like she's really in the hospital anyway. I can see her anytime I want to. I sighed. I knew I was lying to myself, shielding myself from the fear. In truth, I was afraid Evie was going to look like my mother at the end, so I'd spent the last couple of days shut up in my room, avoiding everything and everyone. *Well, everyone except Evie.*

Dad cleared his throat again and flipped on the blinker as he turned off the highway toward town. "Are we going to talk about what happened?"

My stomach twisted. I hadn't told my dad that Evie got hurt while we were searching for Mary's ghost. Or that her ghost had turned out to be something more sinister. I shivered and ripped my gaze from the trees and focused on my hands in my lap. A dozen things ran through my mind.

I was still trying to catch a thought when Dad spoke, "I know why you all were out there."

I glanced his way with my eyebrow raised.

He chuckled. "I grew up here, remember. We all heard stories about the Weeping Bridge." He sniffed. "Couple of us may have even gone out looking for it in our younger, stupider days."

I looked back down at my hands.

"All I want to know is how things went so wrong, Marissa. You're always so careful."

I blinked back the tears that flooded my eyes and shook my head. "Evie slipped. She was on the bridge and we were trying to help Mary."

"The ghost?" My dad cut in. His voice held no note of sarcasm in it and I knew he wasn't judging me, simply asking.

I nodded. "Yeah."

"Did you? Help her?" He turned onto Monroe Street and then into the hospital parking lot. Andy's truck followed us in.

"Yes, and she tried to help me, too."

Dad nosed the pickup into a space and threw the truck into park. He let it idle for a moment and turned to face me across the bench seat. "Listen, I know you're worried that you've somehow broken my trust and that I'm going to put you on lockdown, but that's never how we've operated and I don't want things to change. I know you don't either, so you need to know that I still trust you."

I nodded, blinking back tears. "I trust you, too. And, I promise I won't make you go gray with worry before I graduate."

"I appreciate that." He reached over and patted my shoulder roughly. "Let me know where you're *really* going from now on? It'll make things easier on all of us."

I nodded again and looked out the window at the hospital. It rose two stories, imposing red brick with rectangular windows, a new construction on the street with the Hardees and the city park. Above the double front entry door, a metal awning gleamed in the sun, a metallic dove with an olive leaf in its grasp taking flight from the letters that formed Harris County Memorial Hospital. *Evie's in there.* I sniffed. *Well, her body is anyway.*

Dad and I got out of the truck and made our way to the front entrance with Andy and Tristan following quietly behind. Tristan looked absolutely miserable, and Andy, well, Andy looked hungry. As we went in, an eddy of cool air spun in the space by the doors and some crispy brown leaves followed us, skittering across the tile with a raspy sound. Dad approached the front desk and I hung back with the guys.

"You guys good?" Tristan jutted his chin toward my dad.

I nodded. "We talked on the way over here. We're good."

Andy reached over and pulled at the leg of my jeans.

"Um, what are you doing?"

"Looking for your ankle bracelet."

I smacked his hand away. "I'm not on lockdown. I told you, we're good. What about you two?"

"I don't think my parents even noticed that I wasn't around this weekend. Dad's working on his thesis and Mom's busy with the baby," Tristan shrugged, "but, I doubt they would have bothered to ground me even if they had noticed."

"Andy?"

"They couldn't afford to ground me. I'd eat them out of house and home." He smiled and then grew somber. "Seriously, though, they're worried about Evie. Mom said something about coming down here later on her way to work. Pay her respects, you know."

I bristled. "She's not dead."

Tristan laid his hand on Andy's arm. "We know, Marissa. She'll be fine."

Dad walked over, his hands shoved deep into the pockets of his coat. "She's still in the same room. No change."

We headed toward the elevator. The heels of my boots clicked on the tile floor. With a ding, the doors slid open and we went in, Tristan pushing in the number two. It lit up and the doors slid closed. I heard humming in my ear. I waved my hand to the side.

"I was just trying to provide some music to make your upward journey more enjoyable, St. Louis."

I pressed my lips together. *I can't talk to you right now.*

"That's right!" Evie moved around in front of me. "They can't see me!" She wiggled her eyebrows and moved to the back of the elevator toward Andy and Tristan. I resisted the urge to turn around and just kept my eyes focused on the door. "Too weird, St. Louis. Seriously. I mean, I'm staring *right at them!*" She came over and stood beside me. "It's really not that bad. My body, I mean." When I didn't say anything, she bumped my shoulder. "It's just your average run-of-the-mill medically induced coma. No biggie." She chuckled, but there was sadness in her eyes.

I swallowed around the lump in my throat as the elevator shuddered when it reached the second floor. The doors slid open and we filed out. Dad stopped at the nurses' station and was directed to the end of the hallway. Tucked away behind a row of unused beds along the wall was door number 214. Dad knocked and then opened the door. He walked in and went to the bedside, sitting down in the chair. He pulled the clipboard from its place on the side of the bed and pored over it, his ankle resting on the knee of his opposite leg. Tristan and Andy hovered on the other side of the bed in the small room.

I stood frozen in the doorway.

Evie was asleep, her dark hair pulled into a bun on the top of her head, a hose running from a machine to her mouth, which was kept open by the apparatus on her face. A collar around her neck tilted her head back. Her eyes were closed and dozens of wires ran from machines and the wall to her arms as they pinned down the blanket on either side of her sleeping form. Her face was swollen and bruised and an angry red slash of red bled through the bandage on her forehead.

Oh, Evie.

I felt sick to my stomach and blinked my eyes rapidly, trying to keep the hot tears from falling. I watched as Evie's spirit moved past me and into the room. She stood next to the bed, obscuring my view of my dad. She reached out to touch one of her hands as it lay on the bed. Before she came in contact with it, though, she was pushed away, as if some unseen force was shoving her away from her body. It was like the two magnets I played with when I was little. If I turned them one way, they snapped together, but if I turned them the other, they wouldn't go together, no matter how hard I tried.

She peered down at her body. Then, she looked up at me with wide eyes. "Do you know how I can get back in my body?" Her voice was small and scared.

A tear escaped and I felt my knees buckle. I swooned in the doorway and Tristan turned as I grabbed hold of the doorjamb.

"Whoa!" He strode over to me and put his arm around my middle. "You okay?" he whispered.

Dad hadn't noticed. He was staring at Evie's chart.

"I haven't eaten anything all day," I lied.

"I'm going to take her down to the cafeteria and get her something to eat," Tristan said. He raised his eyebrows at Andy and tilted his head.

"Oh, yeah, awesome, I'm starving." Andy catapulted from his spot by the bed and threw his arm around me from the other side.

"How altruistic of you," I mumbled.

"Mr. Anderson, we're going down to the cafeteria. You want anything?" Tristan asked over his shoulder.

"Maybe a cup of coffee if it's not too sludgy."

I let the boys support me on the way to the elevator and then shrugged them off as we got in. I held the door open for Evie to follow. She got in, looking pensive.

"I'm fine," I said to the quiet elevator. "It was a…shock."

"Yeah," Evie breathed.

When the doors opened, we headed down the hallway to the north wing of the hospital past the gift shop. "You want flowers?" I mumbled as we passed.

"I like that teddy bear." She motioned at a huge pink bear in the window.

Andy led the way to the doors of the cafeteria and grabbed a tray from under the counter. He pulled a salad, chicken strips, a bowl of cereal, a bottle of juice, and a carton of milk from the counter before turning to Tristan. "You want anything?"

Tristan smiled. "What do you want, Marissa?"

"A soda, I guess. Something with lots of sugar and caffeine. Maybe a protein bar?" I added as an afterthought. I scoped out a table in a lonely corner of the cafeteria and made a beeline toward it. Andy paid for everything and came over. "How about this table?" I asked.

"Perfect." He ripped the plastic cover off the salad and began drowning it with ranch dressing.

"Good to see you've decided to go with something healthy," Tristan said, sitting down in the chair next to him.

I pulled out a chair for Evie and waited until she sat down before I perched on the edge of the chair next to hers.

Andy and Tristan regarded me for a moment.

"What's that all about?" Andy nodded toward the empty chair, his mouth full of salad.

"I, um, *we* have something to tell you." I shifted my gaze from one to the other. "Remember how we were talking that night after going to the Dietrich farm? About how I can see things you guys can't and how someone doesn't have to be dead to be a ghost - a spirit without a body?"

"Oh, Marissa, do you think you can see Evie?" Tristan reached over and placed his hand on mine. "Honey, we all want her to be here."

I pulled my hand from under his. I shook my head. "No, it's not like that." I dropped my voice to a whisper. "She's really here, you guys."

Tristan and Andy exchanged a glance. Tristan pursed his lips.

"Tell him thirty-four," Evie said from her chair. She leaned over the table and rested her chin on her folded hands.

"Um, she says thirty-four."

Tristan looked up at me, his face registering surprise.

"What's that supposed to mean?" Andy asked as he dunked a chicken strip into a vat of BBQ sauce. He shoved it in his mouth and shrugged.

Tristan took a deep breath. "I got a thirty-four on my ACT. I found out this morning, but I haven't told anyone."

Andy stopped chewing for a moment, and then he tucked back in and grabbed a forkful of salad. "It means you'll be able to go to any school you want."

"It also means my dad's going to push for me to go to Stanford."

Andy didn't look up. "You're going wherever you need to go. Discussion over." He took a bite and looked up at me. "How'd you know that, Anderson?"

"Evie told me."

Andy snorted.

I shook my head. "You don't believe me."

Evie cocked her head to the side. "Andy still sleeps with a raggedy purple dog he calls Sniffles."

I shared this information and Andy stopped chewing and looked up at the empty chair. He shook his head. "Watching me sleep, Patton? That's pretty high on the stalker scale."

Evie smiled. "He believes you now."

"So, she's just out here *walking around?*" Tristan reached out and waved his hand at the empty space above Evie's chair. His hand brushed her arm and it wisped away from her body, as if he moved a finger across paint that wasn't quite dry. A moment later, her arm snapped back into focus.

I nodded. "Yeah, she's not in her body."

"Well, get back in it, Patton. Seriously, get back in, wake up, and quit drawing out the drama." Andy pointed a chicken strip at her.

Tristan shook his head. "Would you be nice?"

"It's not about being nice. It's about getting her back where she's supposed to be so I can quit worrying about her."

"Softy," Evie said.

"She's tried. Upstairs. I watched and it was like something was pushing her back out."

Andy stared at the empty chair. "We could try shoving her back in."

Evie's eyes darted to the side and she shook her head. "I don't think it works like that. Something did this to me out at the bridge." She shuddered. "When I pushed Mary away from you, Marissa, I-I wasn't inside myself any longer. It was as if I was watching everything from outside my body. I saw my head hit the side and you guys pull me from the water. I watched you drive me to the hospital and the doctors wheel me into the emergency room. I couldn't get back into my body and I didn't know where else to go, so I came to your house."

"It's your house, too," I said and then relayed the conversation to the guys.

"We should go back to the bridge, then," Andy said when I finished.

Evie's eyes grew wide and she shook her head vehemently. "No, I'm not going back there." Her voice had a finality about it.

I shook my head. "She doesn't want to go. Something scared her about that place. You guys didn't see what we did." I shuddered when I thought of the evil that jetted out of Mary's ghost that night. I didn't really like the idea of going back there, either. "Besides, I think we have to have her near her body for her to go back into it. It wouldn't accomplish anything to go out there without her body."

I could see the wheels turning in Andy's head and Tristan saw it, too. He shook his head. "Nope. I know what you're thinking, but I'm not kidnapping a comatose person."

Andy shrugged again. "You have a better idea, Patton?"

"Maybe I have to do something? Maybe I have to help someone. Remember I told you that there was a little girl who needed our help?"

"Yeah, but I don't see how that…"

"It's something!" Evie cut me off.

I sighed and told the guys what she was proposing.

"No way." Tristan shook his head. "After what happened out at the Weeping Bridge, are you mental?"

"Now who's not being nice?" Andy bumped Tristan with his shoulder. "Hear her out."

"Do you even know where the little girl is yet?" I asked.

Evie shook her head.

"How can you find out?"

"I don't know, but I think I have an idea. Remember Sam?"

"Ouija board Sam?"

"Yeah, when we used to talk before he told me things." She looked down at her sweater and picked at the sleeve. Her dark hair fell around her face, masking her features. "He told me that he could see things. Maybe he'll know where she is and how to help her."

"You've seen him?"

Evie shook her head. "No, I…" she stopped and looked up at me. "Go home and pull out the Ouija board and he should come through to you guys like he used to come through to me."

"I thought you said the board was broken."

Andy and Tristan's gazes went from side to side, from me to the empty chair as if they were watching a tennis match but they could only see and hear one player.

"It's not broken anymore. I mean, not the last time I used it. Sam came through to me that time again."

"Why can't you ask him?"

"It doesn't work like that. I can't call him. Well, I don't think I can anyway." She rolled her eyes and stood up. "Get out the Ouija board at home. I'll meet you there."

I stood up, too. "Where are you going?"

She shook her head. "I can't tell you."

"Evie!"

"Goodbye for now," she said. She held up two fingers in the peace sign and backed away slowly from the table.

"Do you think you're fading away? Cause you're not," I called after her. "Come back here and talk to me!"

"Later, St. Louis." She disappeared through the doors. I got up and went to the doors. There was no sign of her. Andy and Tristan came up behind me.

"Did she leave?" Tristan asked.

"Yes," I said. "She said she has to go somewhere and then she'll meet us back at the house. We have to try to contact Sam through the Ouija board when we get there. She said that she thinks he'll know where this little girl is."

"You realize this all sounds completely crazy, right?"

"I'm going to get my dad some coffee and then I'm headed back upstairs. You guys coming?"

"We'll be up in a minute."

I got my dad a questionable cup of coffee and loaded it down with cream and sugar, then passed by the gift shop and ducked in, pulling the pink teddy bear from its perch on the glass shelf by the window. The lady at the counter rang me up and I stood there, shifting from foot to foot as she ran my card.

"Darn thing's been slow all day," she said by way of apology.

I smiled at her. "It's okay." I stared at the cup full of pens on the counter. They had silk flowers taped to the ends, the anti-theft strategy making them look like a bouquet. *What was Evie hiding from me? And what did Sam have to do with all of this? How were we going to get her back into her body? Where was this little girl and how could we help her?*

"Hon?"

I looked up. The lady held my card out to me, her eyes filled with kindness. "Sorry," I mumbled, taking the card from her hand. I put the bear into the crook of my arm and grabbed my dad's coffee from the counter, then headed back upstairs.

CHAPTER 3

It felt strange going into Evie's room at home when she wasn't there. My eyes scanned her bed, hastily made up before we headed out to the Weeping Bridge, her pajama pants thrown over the borrowed bedspread. I swallowed as I knelt down and pulled the Ouija board from under the bed. Carrying it level, I took it to my room, stopping to close the door behind me.

Andy and Tristan stood in the middle of the floor, Andy's face taut.

"What's up?" I asked, dropping to a spot on the rug and placing the box in front of me.

"Do you find this Sam thing weird?" Andy lowered his lanky frame onto the carpet. "I mean, why are we talking to *him?*"

I looked from Andy to Tristan. "I think she believes she needs to help someone."

"Like that will get her back into her body?"

I rolled my eyes. "I don't know." My breath hitched. I couldn't shake the image of Evie's body lying in the hospital bed. "Maybe we all need something to focus on. There's nothing we can do for her from our side." I shrugged.

"You think maybe there's something we can do from *her* side." Tristan sat down, his arms folded across his chest. He shook his head. "What do we do if Sam doesn't know where to find the little girl? Could you try drawing again?"

It doesn't work. I hadn't been able to draw anything but Mary since the night at the bridge. I shook my head. "Let's just, um, try this first?"

"I guess it's as good an idea as any." Tristan stared at me, his eyes watchful.

I felt them boring into me, but I didn't make eye contact. He didn't understand. I *needed* this. I needed something to make me feel normal again. I couldn't stand sitting around, waiting for Evie to wake up.

Andy pulled the board reverently from its ancient box and placed it carefully on the floor between us. He put the planchette in the middle. "Ready?"

"Sure," I rolled my eyes, "this was *so* much fun for me the last time." I glanced around the room as the lights dimmed. Andy and Tristan didn't seem to notice, *but they wouldn't, would they?*

"Come on, Marissa." Tristan nodded toward the board.

I nodded and readjusted myself so that I knelt in front of it. Leaning in, I placed my fingers on the planchette next to Andy and Tristan's. A vibration built around me and my ears popped. *It's okay. This happened last time.* Closing my eyes, I cleared my throat. "We would like to speak to Sam. Is he there?" I felt the planchette respond to my question and I opened my eyes to watch it slide smoothly across the board.

"No." Andy looked up at me. "Someone answered." He raised his voice. "Who is this?"

The planchette swung around, landing on B, then I, T. It jetted up to the letter E and then over to M and back to E.

The sound of giggling surrounded me and I sat back on my haunches. "Hi, Evie."

She appeared by my side, a Cheshire cat grin plastered on her face.

"Will you take this seriously?"

"Hey, Evie," Andy said, looking in the opposite direction of where she was sitting. I pointed and he adjusted his gaze.

"Sorry," she said, "couldn't resist."

"Where were you?"

She shook her head. "Doesn't matter. Come on. Joke's over. Let's call Sam."

I looked at the boys. "She's ready now."

We all placed our fingertips on the planchette, leaving a space for Evie's spectral hands. She placed them on the planchette, her fingertips brushing mine. All of a sudden, a light flashed, sending electricity through me. The muscles in my arms seized and my back went rigid. Images slammed into me, shooting past my mind's eyes so quickly they blurred. I clenched my teeth as one image sped past, then stopped and centered itself in front of me.

A house stood in the middle of a field, with clapboard siding brown with age and chipped concrete steps leading up to a screen door with a rip running down its length. A man stood outside, a can in one hand and a paintbrush in the other, spreading white paint on the surface of the house. He wore a shirt with a red embroidered insignia of a pickaxe and the word *Loroxco* next to it. He whistled, his cheeks blowing out with puffs of air to the tune.

I turned as the screen door screeched open behind me. At first, I almost didn't recognize her. This younger version of Evie's mother was almost pretty, with a flush to her plump red cheeks and black curls cascading down her back. A baby with green eyes perched on her hip as she walked down the steps toward me.

"It looks nice," she said. "Do you think we'll have it done before the winter sets in?"

The man put down the paintbrush and smiled. "Doesn't matter. It's ours now, so we can take as long as we need fixing her up." He squinted, appraising the wall in front of him. "At least it'll look good from the road."

The baby cooed and reached out a pudgy hand to the man.

"Aw, come here, sweetie." He wiped his hands on his pants and reached out to take her, the hood of her little jacket flopping over her face as he cradled her in his arms.

The woman laughed and pulled the hood back, the baby's electric green eyes blinking up at her.

"Evie," I breathed.

Their laughter was the last thing I heard as everything around me went black. A moment later, voices came through, shrill and loud:

"Pull them off!"

"Go get some ice!"

"Marissa!"

I blinked and smiled. "They were so happy."

Andy's face leaned over me. Evie was behind him, pacing back and forth on the carpet. As soon as I spoke, she stopped and looked at me, worry plastered on her features.

I tried to sit up.

Andy held me back. "Hold on. We need to make sure you're not hurt."

I put my hands on the floor to push myself up and cried out from the searing pain that traveled from my hands up my arms. I fell back onto the carpet, my lower lip trembling. Tristan ran into the room, took my right wrist in his hand, and placed a wet rag on my fingertips. I sucked in a sharp breath as the material touched the raw skin. He placed a bag of ice in the rag and brought my other hand over. It took a couple of minutes, but the burning sensation lessened and the cold overtook my digits, numbing them as the iciness spread throughout.

I struggled to sit up. Andy and Tristan knelt on either side of me, supporting my elbows as I sat. Evie continued pacing across the carpet.

"It's okay. I'm okay," I repeated.

"You scared the crap out of us, Anderson. Not cool." Andy attempted a smile, but worry clouded his features.

"Do you feel nauseated? Faint?" Tristan pulled the desk chair over and sat in it, leaning down onto his knees to take one of my hands and then the other. My fingertips were bright pink and white blisters rose on three of my fingers on my left hand and two on my right. I gritted my teeth against the burn.

"No, really, I'm fine." Then, I said it again to make Andy quit looking like that. "I'm fine. What happened?"

Evie stopped pacing and stood, her arms wrapped around her chest. "You reached out to touch the planchette and..."

Andy talked over her. "You reached out to touch the planchette and then you went sort of stiff. Your eyes rolled back in your head and you said Evie wouldn't let go of your hand."

"*Couldn't,*" Evie corrected from her place behind them.

"I don't remember any of that. I was somewhere else."

"You were seeing something?"

I nodded. "But it was different. I mean, usually I can only see the place where I am, you know, how it used to be." I shook my head, trying to clear it. Evie took a step away and my mind became less foggy. "This time, I was somewhere else. A house. And you were there," I nodded at Evie. "Except you were a baby and your mom looked nice. And I think your dad was there. He was painting the house they bought and they were laughing and..." I looked up at her. "They were so happy, Evie."

Something passed across her face, but was gone before I could decipher it. Her brow creased and she leaned against the closet door on the other side of the room. "It was because you touched me."

I shook my head, and then remembered to translate for Andy and Tristan. "She thinks what happened, happened because I touched her."

"It makes sense." Andy looked at the forgotten Ouija board. "Maybe this time we don't let Marissa touch it."

"Couldn't, even if I wanted to," I said, holding up my hands.

Tristan looked back and forth between Andy and me. "You guys can't be serious. We're done with this tonight." He stood up and narrowed his eyes. "She's giving me the look, isn't she?"

I glanced at Evie and smiled. "Yep."

"Fine." He sat back down and leaned over the board. "If it's that important."

"It is," I said softly, "and you can come closer, Evie. You won't hurt me." She shook her head at my suggestion so I stood up and walked over to her. "Come on. See?" I took the ice off my hands and showed her. The blisters had calmed down and the redness was leaving. "It's better, really."

"They were happy?" she whispered, tears glistening in her eyes.

I nodded. "Yeah, they were happy, and they loved you very much."

She blinked and walked over to the board. "Tell them to sit down. We're going to try this again."

"Guys, she wants to try again."

Andy and Tristan sat down flanking the sides of the board and Evie took a spot directly in front of it. They all placed their fingers on the planchette and Evie closed her eyes.

"We are trying to reach Sam," Tristan started. "Is Sam here with us?"

Evie shook her head, her eyes closed.

"Not yet," I said, sitting down on the edge of the bed and cradling my hands in my lap. The burn settled into a dull throbbing. "Evie, you try."

"Sam, it's Evie, remember me?"

The planchette started to move, hesitantly at first, and then in a direct line up to "yes." It slid back to the middle of the board and sat there, waiting.

"What did she ask?"

"She asked if he was here."

"Sam, I need your help. Will you talk to me?"

The planchette indicated "no."

"He won't talk to her."

Tristan's brow furrowed. "Why not?"

I shrugged. "Evie, why won't he talk to you?"

"Shhh," she said. "I think I can hear him. Sam, are you here?"

I looked around the room. Nothing had changed. Suddenly, I heard Andy suck in a breath.

"What's wrong?" I asked.

The sight of the planchette moving with lightning speed from one letter to the other answered my question. Only Evie's hands were on it now, her eyes wide as she watched. I leaned over, trying to read the message. I only caught the last bit before the planchette stopped moving and Evie removed her fingers. She looked up at me with wide eyes.

"He said he could help me, but…"

"You have to meet him."

"Caught that, did you?"

I nodded. "Where?"

"He told me to meet him at City Hall."

I stood up and grabbed my coat from the closet. "Let's go."

Evie shook her head. "Not this time, St. Louis. I'll be back soon." And she was gone.

I threw my coat on the floor. "Crap."

"What's going on?" Tristan said from the carpet. Andy was quietly putting the board back in its box.

"She's going to City Hall to meet Sam."

"And you're not invited to the party?" Andy snorted. "Get used to it, Anderson. Us weird kids get left out of all the good stuff."

I sat down on my bed. A scratching noise came from the middle of the room. I focused on it and tilted my head toward the noise. "What *is* that?"

Andy's brow furrowed and he took the lid off the box. Inside, the planchette moved from G, to I, to S, to A over and over again.

CHAPTER 4

After Andy and Tristan left, I locked the back door and sat down in the corner of the sectional in the living room with my laptop. The aspirin I took earlier was still working and my hands didn't burn much at all. An old episode of FRIENDS played on the TV and a fire was crackling in the fireplace. Every noise made me look up for Evie's return, but it was nearly four hours since she left and she still wasn't home. My dad texted earlier to let me know that he would be home around eleven from the hospital. No new word on Evie. He asked me if I was going to be scared, staying at the house alone, and I told him that I was fine. *I wasn't.*

I opened the maps on my computer and typed in our address. It zeroed in on an expanse of gray space and indicated our house with a little red flag. I zoomed in as far as I could and went up and down the streets of the town, looking for the house I saw in Evie's past. After canvasing the town, I started to venture out into the country surrounding Culvers Grove, Missouri. Each road was intersected by other gravel roads that led off into fields with houses popping up out of the small groves of trees. Nothing seemed to fit. Sighing, I put the laptop beside me on the cushion and slid an old quilt over my legs.

I stared unseeing at the television, my mind turning. If Evie wasn't home in twenty minutes, I would get in my car and drive to town to look for her. Suddenly, lights splashed through the blinds. *Dad's home early.* I threw the quilt to the side and got up to unlock the back door for him. I flipped on the porch light and Grant's Mustang drove around the corner of the house. I closed my eyes. *What am I going to say to him?* Opening the door, I stood on the screened in back porch, my arms wrapped around me and my breath hanging in a cloud on the frigid air.

Grant got out of the car, his eyes locked on me. Closing the car door with a bang, he strode across the driveway and up the three steps to the porch. He stood in front of me, staring at me for a long moment before pulling me to him and wrapping his arms around me. He leaned down and kissed the top of my head, leaving his lips there as he breathed in a huge sigh.

"I've been so worried about you," he said, his voice rumbling in his chest.

I melted into him and the tears came. Suddenly, I was clinging to him, sobs shaking my body as we stood there in the cold night. He held me, rubbing his hand up and down on my upper arm in a soothing motion. The icy air hurt my lungs as I drew in huge gulps of air.

"Come on, let's get you inside," Grant said, supporting me with one arm while he opened the door with the other. He guided me over to the table and pulled out a chair for me.

I sat down and wiped away the tears as he got a large cup from the cabinet and filled it with water. He brought it to me and I took a long drink. I put the cup down on the table and he swung a chair out and sat facing me.

What's wrong with me? I hadn't cried since everything happened on the Weeping Bridge, well, not like this anyway. I had kept it together. Stayed strong, like I did when my mom passed away. I sniffled loudly.

Grant leaned down and caught my gaze. "You okay?"

I nodded and wiped at my nose with the back of my hand. *Classy, Marissa.*

"Here," he reached into his back pocket and pulled out a handkerchief.

I smiled through my tears. "Seriously? Don't you have to use a cane to carry one of those?"

He smiled and held it up to me. "Quit being stupid. Take it."

I took it and used it to wipe my eyes and nose. Then, I folded it and placed it on the table, smoothing the monogrammed H with a fingertip.

"Hey," Grant took my hand in his, "what happened?" His eyes were gentle, full of concern and they made me want to start crying all over again.

"It's nothing." I gauged his face. *How much was I going to tell him?* A quiet moment passed and then another. I cleared my throat. "How much do you want to know?"

Without missing a beat, he said, "Everything."

I nodded. "Everything." *He deserves to know.* With a sigh, I told him about being able to see ghosts, and about how Evie, Andy and Tristan, and I formed the Ghost Hunters Society to find evidence of ghosts. I told Grant about how we investigated at the cemetery and how, after I went to the cave on our property, I could draw places and ghosts. He sat quietly, nodding his head occasionally and watching me with receptive eyes. I told him about going to the Dietrich farm and then going back to help Old Man Dietrich. Then, I told him about how we helped Mary move on with her love, Matthias. My breath hitched and I started crying again when I told him about what happened on the bridge and then how Evie fell in the water trying to save me. I stopped and looked up at Grant. "Say something, please."

"Is Evie okay?"

"She's in a medically induced coma."

"I know, but can you *see* her?"

A wisp of something caught my eye behind Grant's shoulder. Evie stood in the doorway of the kitchen. She shook her head at me.

"Um, no. No, I can't see her." I glanced up at her again and Grant followed my gaze.

"She's behind me, isn't she?"

I pressed my lips together and nodded.

"Does that mean…" he turned to face me, his brow furrowed.

"She's not dead, just not in her body."

Evie came around him and jumped up on the counter. Grant shivered as she walked by.

"So, St. Louis, he's either okay with all of this or he leaves. Which one do you think he'll do?"

I bristled. "He asked. I told him. *Everything.*"

Grant looked from me to the counter. "Um, hi, Evie." She waved her hand.

"She says hi."

He turned back to me and splayed his hands wide. "I don't know what to do here."

"I don't know either."

We were quiet for a moment. Then, he scooted his chair back and stood up. My heart dropped. *He's leaving. This all freaked him out and he's leaving.* I closed my eyes. Then, I felt his hands on mine. My eyes popped open as he pulled me to my feet and wrapped his arms around me. "You'll probably want to look away, Evie," he said as he leaned down and kissed me. His lips were gentle and warm, and his arms were strong. For the second time in the last hour, I let myself get lost in his embrace. The scent of his cologne filled my senses and I felt loved, cherished, and *safe.*

He finally let me go and stood in front of me, his hands shoved deep into his pockets. He regarded me quietly for a moment then smiled. "The answer is yes."

I shook my head.

"You're wondering if I would have asked you out if I'd known about all this beforehand." He reached out and brushed the hair from my cheek. "And the answer is yes."

"Good Lord, St. Louis." Evie jumped down from the counter. "If I stay in here any longer I'm going to throw up. I'll be upstairs."

I smiled. "Evie's leaving."

"Goodnight, Evie," Grant said to the empty space in the kitchen.

"She already left."

He shook his head. "*That's* something I'll have to get used to. How long is she going to be like that?"

"I don't know. She said she can't get back into her body."

"She's tried?"

"Yeah, at the hospital." I dropped my voice. "To be honest, I don't really think she wants to right now."

"Why not?"

I shrugged. "I don't know. She seems different. I feel like she's finally able to do something or be something..." I paused, searching for the word, "special."

"And it doesn't sound like she got to feel that way very much, before."

I nodded. "Yeah, something like that." I pushed in the chair. "Would you like to stay and watch some television with me? Dad's at the hospital and he won't be home for a little while."

"Sure." We walked into the living room and sat down, me in the corner and Grant next to me, his arm draped across the back of the couch behind my shoulders. "So, what are you guys going to do now?"

I leaned into his side. "We wanted to help ghosts. And people." I swallowed. "I don't know what we're going to do now."

"Why does that have to change?"

"It doesn't, I guess. Evie told me about a little girl who needs us."

"Who is it?"

I shook my head. "We don't know. That's what she went to go find out tonight. If we can find this little girl and help her…"

"It's the right thing to do."

I nodded and sighed. "We know. I'm scared, though. What if something bad happens again? Evie was always the brave one."

Grant leaned over and kissed the top of my head again, pulling me into the crook of his arm. "You'll just have to decide which is more important. Staying safe in case something happens, or helping a little girl."

I smacked his hand. "Sounds like you're ready for me to throw myself in the line of danger. Trying to get rid of me?"

He laughed. "Not at all. I trust you and know that you help people even when it's scary. Besides, Evie will still be with you."

I nodded.

"One more question. What happened to your hands?"

I smiled. "We were using a Ouija board and things got a little out of hand."

"I'll say."

"Are you sure you're not going to go home tonight and rethink this entire thing?"

"What entire thing?"

I turned around to face him, my legs drawn up on the couch between us. "This, I'm a weird girl that can see ghosts and goes out ghost hunting and has a ghost for a roommate thing. It's a lot."

He tilted his head and looked at me, his eyes soft. "You're my paranormal princess."

I raised my eyebrow and his cheeks immediately flushed red. I laughed. "One of those things that sounded better in your head?"

"Heh, yeah. Yeah, shouldn't have let that one out."

Headlights splashed through the blinds again.

"Dad's home." A few moments later, I heard the key in the back door and heavy footsteps in the kitchen. "Hey, Dad," I said as he came into the living room.

"Hey, yourself, and hello, Grant." He nodded at us and collapsed in the recliner. He popped the footrest up and leaned his head back, rubbing his eyes with a flannel sleeve. "You'd think they could put more comfortable chairs in those hospital rooms. What are you guys up to?"

"Nothing, Grant came over to check on me."

"I'm glad." He looked at me through tired eyes. "You looked spooked when you left the hospital this afternoon."

"I'm fine. It was terrible seeing Evie looking like that." I shoved away the memory of her lifeless body lying there in the hospital bed.

"He doesn't know?" Grant whispered.

I shook my head once.

"Know what?" my dad asked.

I glanced at Grant. "Um, Grant's transferring to UMKC next semester."

"Oh?" Dad sat up in his chair a bit. "I thought you put in an application for KU?"

Grant sighed. "Non-resident tuition was too much. Maybe next year."

Dad took a butterscotch candy from his shirt pocket and unwrapped it, pulling the wrapper straight between his fingers. "Well, congratulations. We'll sure miss you coming around here, though."

"I'll still be able to come out here and help out around the farm. I'll be home for weekends and breaks." Grant stood up. "I need to get going. Bye, Mr. Anderson."

"Night, kiddo."

I walked with Grant to the back door. "When are you leaving for Kansas City? Will you be around for New Year's?"

He nodded. "Yeah. My dad and stepmom are taking me up the Sunday before the semester starts to get me moved in."

I pressed my lips together.

"Hey," he said, putting a finger under my chin and raising my head to look into his eyes. "I'll text you all the time and I'll be home before you know it. You can come visit me at school, too. Really. It won't be much different than before."

I nodded, but felt a shift inside, like something was breaking. "I know."

He kissed me and then headed out the back door. He waved before he got into his car and drove away.

"How are you?" Dad pulled a mug down from the cabinet and filled it with the cold coffee from this morning. He put it in the microwave and leaned back against the counter, his arms folded.

"I feel like everyone's asked me that, like a million times today. I'm fine. Just tired." Now that Grant was gone, I was antsy to get upstairs and talk to Evie. "I'm going to bed."

"Cranky, too."

I shot a glare and a smile at my dad and headed up to my room. Evie was sitting cross-legged on the futon, her chin resting in her hands.

"How'd it go?" I asked, closing the door behind me. "You were gone a long time."

She sat quietly for a moment as I made my way over to my bed and sat down. When she finally spoke, her voice was quiet. "I met Sam tonight." A shadow passed across her face. "We sat on the porch of City Hall and talked for a long time. He's exactly like I thought he would be."

"What does that mean?"

Evie glanced up at me, her eyes guarded. "I mean that I talked to him dozens of times through the Ouija board and I guess I had a picture in my mind of what he would be like." She stared at the carpet for a minute. "And he was completely what I pictured."

"Why did he want to meet you alone?"

"It's hard for him to talk to the living."

I wrinkled my nose. "The living? That's creepy."

She laughed. "That's just what he calls you."

"And what he should call you, too. Don't forget that you're not dead, Evie."

"Duh. Anyway, he told me how he thinks we can find the little girl. See, we ghosts are able to sense distress in the fabric."

"The fabric?"

"Yeah. Imagine a piece of fabric lying on top of the world. Here," she furrowed her brow and then pulled out the edge of the curtain and held it in the palm of her hand.

"Hold on," I said. "You can *touch* things? Make them move?"

The curtain slipped through her fingers. She pursed her lips at me. "I can, but it takes a lot of concentration," she said pointedly. She took a deep breath and pulled the curtain into her palm again. "The living exist on one side and the dead, or *comatose* people," she added for my benefit, "exist on the other. When a ghost is in distress and attempting to reach out to the other side for help, attention, or both, they press into the fabric and distort it." With that, Evie pinched the curtain in her palm with two fingers and raised it up, creating a tent on her hand. "As a ghost, we can see where those ripples, those distortions, originate from."

"So, if you can find the distortion, we can find the little girl."

She nodded and let the curtain swing back to the window as if it were caught on a slight breeze.

"What time should we head out tomorrow?" I sighed.

Evie smiled a toothy grin. "Any time's good for me."

CHAPTER 5

The next day, we headed out as soon as Dad left for the hospital. Evie sat in the passenger seat, watching through the window as we drove.

"Where should we start?"

She glanced guiltily in my direction. "Promise you won't be mad?"

I raised an eyebrow. "Tell me and then I'll tell you if I'm mad."

"I sort of looked a little on my own last night."

I looked over at her. "When?"

"While you were sleeping."

"So, you don't have to sleep? You don't get tired?"

"It's not that. I get tired, but it feels more like I'm a battery being drained. Sometimes it happens faster than others, but then, I pull back and I feel better."

"Pull back? Is that where you go when you're not around me?"

She nodded. "Yeah, it's hard to explain. I sort of fade out. You know, I close my eyes and I go back to my body. When I open them, I feel like myself again."

"I've felt that draining feeling before. It's like when I see something. I feel like all of my energy is being siphoned off."

"Exactly. Turn here," Evie pointed.

I flipped on the blinker and turned off the highway onto a gravel road that rose between two fields of snow. Checking the gas gauge, I started up the road. "How do you travel from place to place? Are you, like, teleporting?"

She laughed. "No, I have to walk everywhere like I did when I was alive."

"You're still alive," I reminded her under my breath.

We drove along in silence for a minute.

"I know," she said after a long time.

I cleared my throat. "Promise you won't be mad either?" I pulled my purse from the backseat and unzipped it. "Look in the front pocket. There are some papers." I was careful to remove my hand before Evie reached over. I didn't want a repeat of the Ouija board session to occur while I was driving. Nothing like that happened before when I touched other ghosts. I wasn't sure why it was different with Evie, unless it was because she wasn't a *real* ghost. I shoved my thoughts to the side as she pulled the papers out and smoothed them on her lap.

"You're drawing again!"

I nodded. "Yeah, I started drawing this last night after we talked. It was weird. I mean, I hadn't been able to draw anything but Mary since the night at the bridge." I stared out at the road and then glanced down at the picture. "I don't know where it is or *who* it is, but it's for sure connected to *this* little girl, right?"

"This is fantastic, St. Louis!" Her eyes scanned the pages. The first one was of a tire swing hanging from the limb of a tree in the front yard of an old house. The face of a little girl peered out of the front door. It was obscured by the distance from my vision, but she looked to be really young. The next drawing was of a lamp. It had a fabric lampshade and baubles of beads hanging down from the shade. The base was an ornate filigree, and lying scattered in the light from the lamp were several children's books: *Green Eggs and Ham*, *The Light in the Attic*, and *Frog and Toad*.

Evie pulled the next one from behind and gasped. "Holy crap, St. Louis!"

"I know." My mouth pulled straight into a thin line. "It's creepy."

The third drawing was of a doll. Its hair was matted to the side of its head and long curls fell in tangles on the other side. The dress was threadbare and the painted shoes were peeling off. The porcelain face was white with a spider web of cracking crisscrossed along the doll's cheek. The paint of the little bow mouth was crackling and peeling and the nose was broken off on one side. The eyes were the most haunting, though, wide and unseeing.

"Dolls creep me out," Evie said, placing two of the drawings back in my purse. She kept the tire swing sketch out on her lap as we drove.

"I didn't think you were scared of anything. What about the Dietrich farm? The old man made wind chimes out of *doll parts*."

She side-eyed me. "Well, maybe if you weren't so busy being a huge chicken yourself, then you would have noticed that I cut that thing down the last time we were out there. I kicked it under a bush."

"You did what? Evie, some kid's going to find that now. They're going to need therapy."

"It was better than having it hanging in the garden. Besides, I wasn't going to take it in the truck with us. Hey, stop the car!"

I slammed on the brakes and the car fishtailed on a patch of ice. The tires caught the gravel again and I was able to stop. "A little warning would be nice."

"There's something there," Evie said, looking out her window. "I mean, I see a distortion, but there's no house there." She opened the door and got out, climbing the embankment and staring out across the field. I put the car in park and climbed up after her, scanning the field for any sign of ghosts.

"Let's keep looking," I said, dancing from one foot to the other in the snow. "It's cold out here."

She shook her head slowly. "Sorry, yeah, let's keep looking." Her words were slurred and sounded like it took great effort to speak them.

We got back in and I started driving again. "Do you think someone else needs our help?" I jerked my head back, indicating the field we drove away from.

Evie pulled a black curl over her shoulder and played with the ends of her hair. "I honestly don't know. Something was distorting the fabric back there, but I couldn't see anything. You?" She leaned her head back against the headrest and closed her eyes.

"I don't think so." I pushed my eyebrows down and together. "I think we should go back, though, and see if whatever's distorting things needs our help."

"We can do that later." Evie's voice read of exhaustion. "I want to keep looking for the little girl."

I glanced over at her. "Me, too." We drove along the gravel road until we reached a T intersection. I peered over my steering wheel, looking first right then left. The gravel road spread like a long, white ribbon in both directions to a point where it met the horizon and then disappeared over a hill on each side. "Which way now?"

Evie stared out her window and then over me through mine. "I-I don't know." She reached up with a hand and rubbed at her eyes.

"Listen, I don't want you to go away. Stay with me, but stop looking for distortions. It's too much."

Evie nodded and put her head back on the headrest. She pointed out her window. "Try that direction." She sighed loudly and then closed her eyes. "Sorry, St. Louis." A moment later, she was gone.

"Crap," I said. I pulled the car to the side of the road and stared at the empty passenger seat. Putting the car in park, I reached over a hand, testing the air. Nothing sent shockwaves through me, and with this garnering my bravery, I pressed my hand into the seat. Nothing.

Nodding my head, I placed the drawing of the house on the seat where Evie sat and put the car in gear again. I drove as far as I could until the gravel road met with the highway. Turning around, I followed it back to the intersection we arrived at and kept going, with the defrost going full blast in the car. I straightened my fingers and wiggled them, hardly aware that I had a death grip on the steering wheel for the last several miles. I shook my head.

What was Evie trying to accomplish by finding this little girl? For that matter, what am I trying to accomplish? If Evie can't get back in her body, what will happen if her body wakes up? Can it wake up without a soul? How long can her body stay alive? When she wakes up, will Evie still be Evie?

So engrossed was I in the questions floating around in my head, I almost missed the house. By the time I realized that I was looking at the tree with the tire swing, the car nearly passed the residence completely. I slowed down and pulled into the remains of a driveway or farm entrance a little ways down. Hopping out, I yanked the hood of my coat over my head and closed the door quietly. I shoved my hands in the coat pockets and walked in the loose gravel along the side of the road toward the house. It was white, two stories, but small. The front porch dipped a bit as most of the older houses did in the area, and there were wooden scrolls alongside the screen door. A red car was parked in the driveway in front of a detached one car garage. I didn't see another vehicle in the garage, but there were tire tracks in the snow along the driveway from another car or truck. Maybe they weren't home. Or maybe, the mom or dad stayed home with the little girl. I walked along the side of the house, wondering for a moment if I should go up to the door and knock. Two huge trees canopied the backyard and a little kid's slide lay on its side, forgotten in the snow. Suddenly, I heard voices and the slam of the screen door from the front of the house.

I stayed behind the house, peeking out from around the corner. A woman in a long green puff coat came down from the front porch. Her features were pretty and her long blonde hair spilled out over the neck of her coat and halfway down her back. She unlocked the door of the red car and turned back toward the house.

"Hurry up, Hannah! We have to feed Grammy her lunch!"

A little girl in pink snow boots and a purple coat came down the porch steps, struggling to hold onto the doll in her arms as she negotiated the steps.

There was some discussion I couldn't hear as the woman buckled the little girl into the back seat and then the mother emerged, her lips drawn into a thin line. The little girl began shrieking and the mother slammed the back door of the car. She ran to the front of the house before getting in the car again. The little girl's screaming ramped up a notch as the mother put the car in gear. Her car's belts squealed in protest, and then she backed out onto the gravel road, roaring off in the opposite direction from where my car was parked.

When they were out of sight, I hurried around the side of the house and glanced up at the porch. There, slumped against the front door was the doll the little girl had been carrying. It watched me with wide open eyes as I walked up the steps toward it. It was the doll from my picture. I couldn't imagine why the little girl was holding onto it and shuddered as I leaned down to touch the edge of the frayed dress.

A moment later, I was drenched in sunlight, the rays beating down on me unhindered by the limbs of the huge tree in the front yard. I turned to look and found a much smaller version of the tree, its trunk spindly and new. Laughter spread around me. A little girl with ringlet curls of brown hair ran around the yard, laughing as she looked at a doll sitting at attention on a wrought iron chair.

"...*Mache schnell die Aeuglein zu, So findest du deine Ruh...*" the little girl sang as she skipped around the doll. There was a flash and the scene was gone.

I shook my head, attempting to gauge how much time had passed by how drained I felt. The day was taking on the grayness of the too-early evening through the winter months. I grabbed my phone from my pocket and checked out the time. It was almost four in the afternoon. I'd lost hours. Sighing, I put my phone back in my pocket and made my way back to my car. When I got in, I laid my head back and rested it on the seat. I felt drained, but not as bad as usual. After a few minutes, I decided it was safe to drive and put my car in gear. As I passed the house, I paused to take note of the address on the mailbox: 1290 County Road 243.

CHAPTER 6

"Hey, St. Louis. You're never going to believe this."

I rolled over as Evie walked in the door. Stretching, I squinted at the clock on my nightstand. "What time is it?"

Evie shot me an impatient look as she sat down on the futon.

The clock told me that it was around three o'clock in the morning. I groaned and struggled to sit, drawing my legs up and pulling the comforter snugly around my shoulders. I cleared my throat. "You were gone a long time."

"Yeah, I stopped off at the hospital."

"You did?" I wiped the sleep from my eyes.

She nodded. "Your dad's still there."

I felt a needle of jealousy, but dismissed it quickly. "He stays with you every night."

"He should stop."

"You had something to tell me?" I said, the edge of irritation clipping my words.

She considered me for a moment. "I can see how you're feeling. You're mad."

I waved a hand in her direction and then plunged it back under the covers.

"No, seriously. I can see a sort of color coming off you when you're upset. It's less now, but a moment ago, it was bigger." She tilted her head at me. "Are you mad because your dad's paying more attention to me than you?"

I closed my eyes, struggling to keep my breathing even. *She can see if you're upset,* I reminded myself.

"The color is even brighter now. That's it, isn't it?"

I threw the covers off and slid my feet into my tattered slippers. The ears of the bunnies flopped lazily to the side as I wrapped my fluffy robe around me. "I'm going downstairs to make some hot chocolate. Want to come?"

Evie nodded and walked behind me as I descended the stairs. She sat down at the table while I pulled a mug out of the cabinet. "He's just worried."

I slammed the cup down on the counter and spun around. "Jesus, Evie! We're all worried about you! You're lying in a hospital bed and you don't seem to care!"

Evie looked like I struck her. She stared down at the table. "I've tried to get back in my body…" she trailed off.

"Have you?"

She glanced up at me.

"Really? Have you really tried to get back into your body or are you enjoying all this attention you're getting all of a sudden?" My chest rose painfully up and down as I talked.

Evie stood up. "I don't have to stay here and take this."

"What are you going to do? Where are you going to go?"

"I have places," she mumbled.

We stood there for a moment, uncomfortable silence stretching out in the gap between us.

"I'm worried that you know how to get back in your body, but you're happy that now you can do the things that you always wanted to do and people are worried about you, for once, and now you don't want to get back into your body. Because, you think it will all go back to how it was before you got in that accident."

She looked up at me and narrowed her eyes. "Green's not a good color on you." And, she was gone.

I stomped my foot on the floor and one of the rabbit's eyes went rolling across the linoleum. That caught me funny and I started laughing. I laughed until I cried and then I cried until I started hiccupping. When I finished cycling through the gamut of emotions, I put the mug back into the cabinet and turned up the heat before heading back upstairs to my bedroom. I started to close the door, but then left it open a bit, *in case she comes back.*

***

The next morning dawned bright. It was a couple of days before New Year's Eve and the sunny weather looked like it would hold out for another week or two. The house was toasty warm. I would have to turn the thermostat down before Dad got home. He probably already knew I turned it up, though. He possessed some sort of radar for that thing. I wandered downstairs and had my hand on the dial when I heard a voice behind me.

"I can't."

I whirled around, my hands in front of me in a wild chopping action, a sound somewhere between a strangle and a hiccup escaping from my lips.

Evie sat on the couch. She raised an eyebrow in my direction. "Would you please take a self-defense class? Unless you're trying to make the intruder pee himself from laughing. If that's what you're going for," she threw two thumbs up in the air, "you're golden."

I put my hands down and glared at her. "Shut up."

She followed me into the kitchen and watched from the counter as I got down a bowl and my favorite cereal. We were almost out. I'd have to go shopping soon.

I sat down at the table with the milk. "You can't what?" I asked as I poured.

Evie looked out the window a moment. "Your dad's home." She flipped on the coffee pot.

A moment later, I heard the gravel crunch under his tires.

"You can't what?" I repeated.

She regarded me for a moment. "I can't get back into my body. I told you that."

"And I told you that I think it's more about not wanting than not being able to."

The back door opened and Dad came in, reaching out to hang his coat on the peg. "It's hot in here. What do you have the thermostat up to?" he asked as he walked through the kitchen to the living room to check. "Good grief, Marissa. You don't need to have it up this high."

"Hey, Dad," I mumbled into a spoonful of cereal.

"You're sad now. I can see the indigo coming off you."

"Stop doing that." I shot a glare at Evie.

"What?" Dad asked. He stood under the archway and unbuttoned the sleeve of his flannel shirt before rolling it up on his arm.

"Nothing. Any change in Evie?"

He shook his head. "I thought she heard me earlier. I thought I saw her hand twitch, but I guess it was just wishful thinking." He looked up, bags under his eyes and his hair ruffled. "I need to take a shower and get some things before I head back over there."

"Mmmhmmm," I mumbled, reading the back of the cereal box.

He didn't leave. I looked up.

"My mom came to the hospital," Evie said. "He's upset about that but he doesn't want to tell you."

What are you, psychic now, too?

"No, not psychic." Evie's voice was full of sadness.

I turned to look at her.

Dad came into the room and stood in my line of vision. "Marissa, I'm worried about you."

Evie leaned around him. "Told ya."

I rolled my eyes at her.

"I know you don't like me to worry about you, but honey, I don't think you've processed what happened at the bridge that night. Your friend was in an accident and she's at the hospital fighting for her life and you don't seem to have any desire to see her."

"Yeah," Evie said. "You're being kind of a jerk."

I narrowed my eyes. "I don't want to go visit her because she's not there. She's here. In this house. Right behind you."

Dad furrowed his brow and turned to look at the counter. "What do you mean she's *here?*"

I sighed. "Come sit down?"

He poured a cup of coffee and then pulled out a chair, settling his lanky frame into it with a grunt. His eyes were expectant.

I pushed my cereal bowl away. "Remember how I told you that we were at the Weeping Bridge to help Mary's ghost?"

He nodded.

"Well, I know you want to trust me so I need to tell you something."

"At this rate, you should get 'I Can See Ghosts' printed on a t-shirt to save time," Evie said.

I ignored her. "So, for a long time now, I-I've been able to *see* ghosts."

Dad nodded again.

I waited for him to say something and when he didn't, I plunged on. "Since I was little I was able to see things that weren't really there. I've seen Grandma and others. When I came here, it got more intense. I started seeing things all the time. Before we moved, Andy, Tristan and Evie used to try to find evidence of ghosts and when they found out that I could see them, I started going with them on their ghost hunts. We also found out that we could help the ghosts move on. We went to a farm and helped Theodore Dietrich move on so he could be with his wife and we helped Mary reunite with her love, Matthias. That's where we were when Evie got hurt." I cleared my throat. "And even though her body's in the hospital, her spirit is *here*."

Dad took a long sip from his coffee cup, the steam whirling around his face. He pulled a butterscotch candy from his shirt pocket and stared at it.

"He cried about your mom last night." Evie came over and stood next to my dad. "He cried because he's watching me waste away in a hospital bed like he watched her. And, he feels so helpless. Like he can't do anything again."

Tears sprang to my eyes. I got up and threw my arms around my dad's neck. He wrapped his arms around me and squeezed me tight against him. I looked up at Evie. She had tears in her eyes.

A minute later, Dad leaned back, wiping at his eyes with the back of his hand. He coughed and cleared his throat as he got up to refill his already full coffee cup, his back to me.

I sat back down and watched him. "Evie says you cried for Mom last night."

His shoulders drew up tensely and he froze, the coffee pot held above his cup. He sighed and poured a bit into the cup before placing the pot back on the maker. "Have you ever seen...*her?*" he asked without turning around.

I spoke around the lump forming in my throat. "No, Dad, Mom's gone." I rushed on. "She's happy. The only ones that I see are people that still need my help. Mom's happy wherever she is."

Dad dropped his head, shaking it back and forth. He turned around and leaned against the counter. "This is real, isn't it?"

"Yes." Hot tears rushed to my eyes. I could tell by the way that he was looking at me that he believed me, believed *in* me. My chest hurt with the relief that came crashing in on me. "It's real and Evie's here."

"Right here?" He pointed at the floor.

"On the counter next to you."

Dad turned and looked at the empty counter. He reached out and then brought his hand back to rub his chin. He sighed audibly.

"Tell your dad that I saw him make the deal. I want him to find him."

"Evie says she wants you to find him. Who does she want you to find?"

"Her dad." He came back over and sat down at the end of the kitchen table. He rested his elbows on the glossy wood top and tented his fingers. He pressed his index fingers to his mouth and regarded me. "Last night, one of the nurses came to get me because Genevieve's mom was at the front desk. She heard about Genevieve and wanted to see her."

Evie looked at an imaginary watch on her wrist. "Only two days after her daughter is in a serious accident. Sounds about right."

Dad went on. "I went downstairs and saw her at the counter. She was frantic. The front desk already called the police by the time I got there. When she saw me, she went ballistic. I swear, if the counter hadn't been between us, she looked like she would have clawed my eyes out. After she was asked to leave, I saw her standing outside the doors, smoking a cigarette."

"You went out there, didn't you?" I asked.

"Of course, he did." Evie rolled her eyes.

Dad nodded. "I did. I tried to think about if I was in her place and you were in the hospital, Marissa. I would do about anything to see you."

"They made a deal," Evie said.

"What's the deal?" I asked.

Dad looked at me. "She was there? Genevieve? She saw me talking to her mother?"

"I think so."

"I was."

"She was."

"So, she can talk to you? Can you hear her *and* see her?"

"Dad."

He shook his head. "Sorry." All the tiredness left his eyes and they blazed like they did when he was working on a good case. "Anyway, when I went out to talk to Genevieve's mother, she'd calmed down enough to talk to me and she said something really interesting." He paused and looked at me. "Does Genevieve want to tell you?"

Evie sat down next to me. "I want to show you, St. Louis. That way, I'll know if it's true."

I sighed and rubbed my sore palms under the table. "Remember what happened last time?"

She nodded, but didn't break eye contact. "Please, St. Louis. I need to know if what she said was true."

I drew a deep breath and turned to my dad. "Evie wants me to find out something. Sometimes when I touch a ghost or am in a place where something happened, I can see glimpses of what happened in the past."

Dad rubbed his hands over his eyes. "This is a lot. She wants to know if her mother sent him away, doesn't she?"

Evie nodded.

"Her mom always told her that her dad left them. She said he didn't love them anymore," I said.

"I believe her," Dad said. "I believe her mom."

"Evie doesn't," I said.

"Of course, she doesn't," Dad said, almost to himself. "Why would she believe her mother? She lied to her all her life."

"If I can see the moment her dad left, I'll be able to tell if her mom is telling the truth."

"What does that change?" Dad asked. "I mean, either way, he left his wife and a baby." Disdain coated his voice. "You don't do that. No matter what, you don't leave the ones you love."

"She deserves to know." My resolve solidified. "And, I can give her that, Dad. I can see what happened and tell her. *You* would want to know, wouldn't you?"

Dad looked from me to the empty chair where Evie was sitting. Finally, he nodded. "What happens next?"

"I'm going to reach out and touch her and I should be able to see a vision, a memory."

"She was a baby."

"But, she saw it. It's in her somewhere."

He nodded. "You sound hesitant to do this. Why?"

I swallowed. "The last time we made contact, my fingers got burned. It hasn't ever happened like that before. I think it's because she's not really a ghost.

She's more powerful somehow because she's more alive than the other ghosts I've come into contact with."

"Any chance this is safe?"

I laughed. "Andy and Tristan said that the last time this happened, I went rigid, like electricity was passing through me. They said my eyes rolled back in my head and I was out for a few minutes."

Dad stood up. "No, Marissa, I can't let you do this."

I looked him dead in the eye. "You know as well as I do that I'm going to do it either way. Now, you can either stay to watch or Evie and I can go up to my room and we'll do it anyway."

He stared at me for a moment. "You remind me so much of your mother." The corners of his mouth turned up and I knew it was a compliment. "I'll stay."

"Good," I said. "Let's go in the living room. That way if I fall, I won't hurt myself." I walked out of the kitchen with more confidence than I felt.

CHAPTER 7

Dad sat in the recliner, leaned over his folded hands, his elbows resting on his knees. "You're sure you'll be okay?"

"I'll be fine," I responded from my spot in the corner of the couch. "Whatever happens, though, you have to sit there. Don't touch me because it will pull me out of the memory."

Dad sighed as I tucked pillows around on all sides and a blanket over my legs. Evie sat on the edge of the cushion next to me.

"You're sure this will work?" she asked. "I mean, you've never gone in to look for a specific memory."

"I think if you're thinking about it, I can tap into that," I said.

She looked at me for a moment. "I don't want to hurt you."

"I'll be fine." I held up my hands. "See? Not a mark. They healed really quickly. I want to help, Evie. Put your hand here." I indicated the large pillow to my right with a nod of my head.

She hesitated, and then placed her hand, palm up, on the pillow.

I closed my eyes and concentrated on tapping into the memory of Evie's dad leaving. Reaching over, my hand hovered over hers for a second and then I dropped it into her palm.

The pain was immediate and excruciating. I cried out as my body tensed, every muscle contracting at once. My palm was on fire where it came into contact with Evie's and it felt like my hand was melting off its bones. Then I saw it. The living room vanished and I was standing in front of the little house I saw the last time. The paint was finished on the front of the house and the trim was painted a sweet green color. There were flowers planted in the boxes flanking the front porch steps and the walk to the porch was paved with bricks.

I spun around as gravel churned under tires, the sound carrying up to the house. A brown truck fishtailed into the driveway and as soon as it skidded to a stop, a man jumped out. It was Evie's dad, but he looked different from the last time I saw him. He was unshaven and his hair was wild around his face. His shirt was covered in dirt and his pants hung loosely on his body. A gauntness haunted his features and his eyes were deep set and shadowed. He paused by the front of the truck and leaned over, his body heaving as he threw up. The liquid splashed up onto the tires. He wiped at his mouth with the back of his hand and strode across the driveway to the front door. With a yank, he pulled it nearly off its hinges. It swung in a broken arc over the steps and he stepped through the open door. I followed him into the house.

He stood, breathing heavily in the living room before crossing it and staring into the playpen in the corner. A toddler version of Evie looked up at him with green eyes, cooing excitedly and reaching up with fat little hands toward her dad. He was leaning over to pick her up when Evie's mom came into the room.

"What are you doing?" Her voice was shrill.

Evie's father turned to her, his eyes wild. He walked over to her and took her shoulders in both his hands. "Please, please, Tammy. We have to leave. *Now.*"

Evie's mother shook out of his grasp. "Have you been drinking?"

A low growl escaped his lips and he threw his head back. "I haven't touched a drink for three years!" He leveled his gaze at her. "I am not drunk or crazy. This *thing*," he gestured wildly at the front door, "is killing me from the inside out! I don't know what's happening, but it has to stop!" He stopped and closed his eyes. He looked like he was listening to something. Then he shook his head. "Tammy, please," he said in a level voice when he opened his eyes, "we have to get out of here."

Evie's mother planted her feet. "We just bought this house, Jeff. We can't up and leave it."

"I can't stay here! I'm afraid I'm going to do something…hurt someone! What if it's you? Genevieve?" He raked his hands through his hair. "I couldn't live with myself! I'm taking her and we're leaving. You have the choice to go with us or stay."

Something shifted in Evie's mother's eyes. She moved, insinuating herself between her husband and her child. "You are not taking her," she spat.

A guttural yell shook the house as Evie's dad raised his fists above his head, swinging them down on either side of her mother's head. His fists stopped mere inches from making contact. Evie's father looked at his hands as if they'd betrayed him, lowering them slowly. He backed away, tears filling his eyes. "I'm so sorry," he whispered. "I'm so sorry."

Evie's chin quivered and her wide eyes spilled tears out onto her chubby cheeks. She opened her mouth and started screaming, her face screwed up in fear and anger.

Evie's mother recovered and found her voice. She picked Evie up out of the playpen and held her protectively against her chest. She looked at Evie's father and quietly said two words, "Get. Out."

"Babe, you know that wasn't me. I've never raised a hand to you. It's that *thing,*" he spat, his eyes darting to the front door again.

Her mother took another step toward her father. "Get out," she repeated. "Get out now."

He took a step back, his eyes searching hers. "I'm so sorry. Please come with me. Please?" His voice trembled and his shoulders shook. "I can't leave you behind. It's too dangerous now. We have to leave this place. It's only going to get worse!"

Evie's mother kept taking one step and then another toward him, backing him toward the front door. "Get out. Leave."

"Please," he cried, spittle falling from his mouth onto his chin as he took another step back. He made contact with the screen door and stopped. "Please, don't do this."

Evie's mother's voice was low but dangerous. "Leave, and don't you ever come back here." She pushed at his chest with the hand that wasn't holding the screaming Evie. "Leave!" She shoved him backwards onto the porch. When her hand left his chest, it took with it a tendril of black smoke. It stretched from his chest, wrapping around her hand, caressing her wrist before plunging back onto Evie's father. Tammy shook her hand, making a fist at her side.

Evie's father stood on the front porch, a broken man as tears poured down his cheeks. "I love you, Genevieve," he said as the front door was slammed in his face. He slumped to his knees on the top step. "No, no, no," he cried.

I stood somewhere in between the wall, able to see the drama unfolding on both sides of the door. Evie's father knelt on the front porch crying while Evie's mother pressed her back into the locked door, sliding down until she was seated on the floor, cradling Evie in her arms as she rocked back and forth, shaking with sobs. Several minutes later, Evie's father made it to his feet and stumbled to his truck, an inky black mist tangled around his feet as he walked. He backed out, pausing to look back at the house before driving off, a cloud of dust following his truck. Evie's mother stood up, placed Evie back in the crib and went into the kitchen, pulling a bottle of whiskey from a hiding place on the pantry shelf. She took a long draw from the bottle, tears streaming down her face as the afternoon sun bathed her in buttery light. She sat there drinking as Evie's cries filled the house.

The scene flashed with light and then I was back. I cried out in pain, yanking my searing hand from Evie's and rolling to my side, cradling my burned hand. Dad jumped up from his spot on the chair and helped me to my feet. He practically carried me to the kitchen where he ran cold water into a large bowl in the sink and placed my hand into it. The water felt like knives stabbing my palm and tears streamed down my cheeks. The skin was an angry, shining red, and an enormous blister was already rising on the bottom of my hand.

"Hold it there for ten minutes," Dad said, his voice calming. "Just breathe, Peanut."

"Evie, are you okay?" I asked, my voice shaking. I tried to take a deep breath, but a sob pushed the air from my lungs.

She hovered near the counter, clasping her hands together and moving from foot to foot, her face full of concern. "I'm fine, St. Louis. Oh my gosh," she whispered, looking down at my hand. "Oh my gosh, I'm so sorry."

I took another deep breath. Dad handed me a couple ibuprofen and I swallowed them dry. He took my wrist and lifted the hand out of the water. Looking at my palm, he turned it from side to side. "It's going to hurt for a while, but I don't think it's too serious. I'm going to get some gauze. Wait here."

I placed my hand back in the water, wincing as knives stabbed it again. A few minutes later, the cool water soothed most of the immediate burning and the ibuprofen was beginning to take the edge off a bit. Dad tore a leaf off the aloe plant that sat on the windowsill above the sink and squeezed it, draining the leaf of aloe that dripped down onto the palm of my hand. He wrapped it gently with the clean white gauze and hooked it with a piece of white medical tape. "There," he said, "we'll keep an eye on it so it doesn't get infected."

"It won't have time to get infected," I said. The strength left my legs and I sat down hard in one of the kitchen chairs. "This will be gone by tomorrow."

Dad raised his eyebrows. "Do you want something to drink?"

"A soda would be nice. You might have to open it for me, though."

Evie stood uncertainly in the doorway. She was still rocking from foot to foot.

"I'm going to be fine, Evie."

She nodded her head, but her face didn't change and she didn't seem comforted at all.

Dad handed me a soda and I picked it up with my non-bandaged hand. I took a long drink, relishing the coolness in my throat.

"Did you find out what you were looking for?" Dad asked.

I nodded. "Come here, Evie." I kicked out the chair next to me for her. "Sit down."

She sat next to me, her brow furrowing as she looked at my hand.

"She was telling the truth," I said quietly. "She made him leave." I relayed the story of what I saw in the vision.

Evie's gaze never left my face as I talked. She chewed on her bottom lip when I finished.

"Say something?" I asked.

She shook her head.

Dad cut in. "Genevieve, dear, you know this since apparently you were privy to the conversation last night, but your mother and I made a deal. If she could help me find your father, I would get her in to see you. Does that sound like something you're willing to do?"

Evie moved her head up and down slowly, her eyes far away. "Yes, yes, I want you to find my dad and I want my mom to come see me."

I told him what she said.

Dad shook his head once and looked at me. "Then, that's exactly what we're going to do."

"How are you going to find him?" I asked.

"I'm not going to have to do much. Apparently, her mother's known his whereabouts for a long time."

Evie pressed her lips together. "I'm tired," she said abruptly. "Thanks, St. Louis," she said a moment before she faded away.

"She left. I don't think she knew that," I said to my dad.

"Sadly, I think she did. In her heart of hearts, she knew her mother had been keeping a secret from her."

I sat there for another minute. "So, what do we do now?"

"Well," Dad said, getting up, "I'm going to go take a shower and then I'm going to head back to the hospital. I'll get in contact with Genevieve's mom and dad from there. Are you coming with me?"

I shook my head. "There's something else I need to tell you."

Dad leaned back in his chair. "Okay."

I told him about Evie not being able to get back into her body and how she wanted to help a little girl. "She thinks it will help." There was no conviction in my voice.

Dad was quiet for a long time. "Sometimes we latch on to the things we *can* control. Especially when we're feeling helpless." He stood up. "That's why I'm going to the hospital."

"Why?"

"Because, some part of her is still in that hospital bed and it's what I can do." He leaned over and kissed me on top of the head. "Get the guys together and go help that little girl."

CHAPTER 8

"What are we going to say?" Andy glanced over at me as he negotiated the slushy gravel roads to the house.

"I think we need to let her mother know that we're here to help. We can tell her about what we've experienced and how we've helped in the past. Turn here," I directed.

"We don't have a great track record," Andy commented. "The last time we went on a ghost hunt, we ended up with one of us in a coma."

"She'll have heard about that, Marissa," Tristan said from the middle of the bench seat. "Everyone in this town has heard about Evie."

"Going back to school's going to be a real trip. Everyone's going to want to know the *real story*." Andy shifted as the wheels of the truck tossed up loose gravel. "What are we going to tell them?"

I sat looking out the window, mulling over what they were asking. *I wish Evie were here. It would be easier if we could ask her what she wants us to tell everyone.* I hadn't seen her since the early morning hours. "I think we tell people that Evie was in an accident. She slipped on ice and hit her head on the bridge. It's the same thing we told the doctors."

"But, that's not really what happened, is it?" Tristan furrowed his brow. "Do you feel like you can talk about what happened now?"

I pressed my lips together. "I'm sorry. Sometimes I forget that you guys can't see what I can." I recounted the story of what I saw in Mary's house and how I followed her ghost down to the bridge where the Union soldiers hung her beloved Matthias. I told them about how she tried and tried to pull him up, her hands bloody on the rope. "Then, she looked at me and her features changed. They turned," I searched for the word, "*evil.* Her eyes were black and when she opened her mouth, there were all of these pointed teeth. Mary reached out and tried to push me back off the bridge, but it wasn't Mary. It was something much darker. Much more dangerous. That's when Evie ran up and pushed it away from me. When she did, she lost her balance and fell into the water."

"She could see Mary?"

"I asked her and she said that she couldn't see Mary, but she could see something and she said it scared her to death."

"Where did it go?"

"I think when Evie shoved Mary's ghost, whatever it was inside of her got pushed out of Mary's ghost. It stood on the end of the bridge and looked at me." I shuddered at the memory. "Then it disappeared."

"What happened to Mary?" Tristan asked.

"She helped me hold onto Evie before you and Andy came to help and then she walked away with Matthias."

"Oh." Tristan pulled at the cuff of his sweater.

The cab of the truck was quiet for the next few minutes.

"Turn left here," I said. Up ahead, I could see the house as we drove along the road. The red car was parked in the driveway and a white work truck was beside it. Andy pulled into the driveway and stopped alongside the car. We all got out and stood looking at the house. Something pulled at me, but I couldn't quite put my finger on the location or source of the feeling.

"You should do the talking," Andy said. He pulled his hood on and we walked to the front porch, our breath hanging on the icy morning air.

The guys flanked me as I stood in front of the door, my hand raised to knock. I took a deep breath and rapped sharply once, twice. It was quiet inside and then we heard the heavy steps of boots approaching the door. A man's face peered at us through the small glass window at the top of the door and then I heard the lock flip.

He opened the door. "Do you kids need some help?"

I raised my hand. "Hi, we're from the local high school and…"

"We aren't interested. Have a nice day," the man said, turning away and beginning to close the door.

"He thinks we're trying to sell him something," Andy said from the side of his mouth.

"Excuse me, sir, but we stopped by to see if there was someone in this house who, um, who needed help?" The words felt stupid and wrong falling from my mouth. *What did you expect? He would open the door and swoon over this group of high school kids who were there to cleanse his house of ghosts?*

The man hesitated and looked at us again. "Someone that needs help?"

A little girl with blonde curls peeked out from behind the man's leg. I smiled and waved at her and then turned my attention back to her father. "Um, yeah. See, we're a group that…"

I was cut off by the little girl's squeal. "Swing!" She pointed behind us and I turned to see Evie swinging back and forth on the tire swing. Her long black hair billowed out behind her and she swung back and forth. She smiled and wiggled her eyebrows. "You'll have to come back and talk to the mom. He won't listen." She held out her hand and beckoned to the little girl.

The little girl slipped out from behind her dad's legs and started out onto the porch. Her little hands reached out toward Evie and the swing.

"Evie's here," I said to Andy and Tristan.

Before the little girl could get to the steps, her father scooped her up. He held her on his hip and stared out at the swing, then looked around.

There's not even a breeze. He's wondering how on earth that tire can be moving.

"Listen, we're eating breakfast in here and I have to get to the job site. I don't think we need anything you're selling today. Thanks," he said, closing the door behind him.

Evie hopped down off the swing. "We should head down the road a way and wait for him to leave. The mom will talk to you."

We piled in the truck again and I directed Andy to the abandoned driveway I parked in the day before. Evie met us there. She sat perched on a stump, her green leggings bright in the morning sunlight. Andy put down the tailgate and we hopped up and sat in a row facing her.

"How's your hand, St. Louis?"

I pulled the gauze back and showed her. "It's better."

"You should quit burning our friend, Patton."

She shot Andy a nasty look and then turned her eyes to me. "I'm really sorry about that. I-I had to know."

I nodded. "I know. Can I tell them what happened?"

Evie nodded.

I told the guys what happened that morning and then I told them exactly what I saw when I went into the memory.

Evie sat quietly when I finished. "What do you think my father was so afraid of?" she asked finally.

"Why was her dad so scared?" Tristan echoed her question.

"I don't know. Something really had him shaken, though. He seemed like he was afraid of something inside himself."

"What if it was the same thing that was inside Mary's ghost?" Tristan asked.

None of us spoke for a minute.

"That doesn't make any sense," I said.

"Sure, it does," Andy said. "If something bad took over a ghost, it stands to reason that it could take over anything."

I shook my head. "It wasn't the same. There was something inside Mary making her do things."

"Like trying to shove you over the edge of the bridge," Tristan said.

I nodded. "Right, but this, *this* felt like something attached itself to Evie's dad. That black mist around his ankles was swirling around him. Like it was, I don't know, *influencing* him somehow."

Tristan pulled out his phone. He typed something in and then scrolled through a page while we watched. He looked up. "Oh, um, yeah, I was looking up an article I read a while ago. It was about how there are pockets of evil in places and sometimes parts of that evil can attach to living people. It influences them to do things. Things they would never do on a regular day."

"That sounds like a movie."

"Exactly! Do you remember the movie *The Amityville Horror*?"

Andy and Evie nodded. I sat still.

"You've never seen it?" Tristan asked.

"She's the Queen Chicken," Evie said.

"Shut up. I don't like scary movies."

"Read the book?"

I shook my head.

"In the 1970s, a man named Ronald DeFeo Jr. shot and killed his entire family: father, mother, two sisters, and two brothers. He pled insanity and was sentenced to life in prison. He said he heard voices telling him to kill his family. After that, another family moved in and said that they were terrorized by paranormal activity. There were claims that the father of the family started to take on a resemblance to Ronald and they only spent twenty-eight days in the house before they fled and left all their belongings behind. The movie is about the house."

"Wow," I breathed.

"Yeah," Tristan said, "there are many stories about places that have seen such evil holding onto that energy. That energy can then attach itself to people."

"Do you think something like that happened to my dad?" Evie asked.

"I don't know," I said, "but, Evie, whatever that black mist was, when your mom touched your dad's chest, it touched her, too."

"Maybe that's why she's always been so awful," Evie said, hopping down off the stump. "He's leaving. Let's go."

I sat there for a minute. "Do you think that's what happened to Evie's dad? He was influenced by something evil?"

Tristan shook his head. "I don't know. It's the best theory I have, though."

"Come on," Andy said, standing up. "Let's go try this again. You think you can do the talking again, Anderson, or do you need some cue cards this time?"

We got in the truck and drove back up the road to the driveway. This time, the white truck was gone and the little red car remained. Andy parked and we all walked back to the front porch steps. I knocked on the door again and a moment later, a woman opened it. "Yes?" she asked through the screen door.

"Hi, my name's Marissa and this is Andy and Tristan, and," I stumbled, "um, we've come to offer some help."

The woman's eyebrow knit together. "Help for what?"

"We have reason to believe that something is happening in this house that is scaring your little girl."

The mother regarded us for a moment. Her eyes registered something unreadable and then she plastered a smile on her face. "Listen, I'm not sure what you're doing here, but we're fine."

The little girl ran to the door and waved. "Hi," she said.

"Hi, there. My name's Marissa."

"Her name is Hannah," Evie said in my ear. "Elizabeth, after her great aunt."

"Hi, Hannah Elizabeth," I said.

The little girl smiled and the mother placed a protective arm around her daughter's shoulders. "How did you know her name?"

"I know this sounds crazy, ma'am, but my friends and I look for evidence of paranormal activity, um, ghosts, and we were led to your house because we believe something is happening here." I tried to convey calm and confidence, but I began chewing on my bottom lip and wringing my hands. "We're here to help," I said in a small voice.

"Mommy? Mommy, can I play with the nice lady?" She pointed past me. "She's swinging again."

The young woman looked past me at the tire swing going back and forth in the still morning. Her face blanched. She leaned down and looked at her little girl. "Hannah, honey, why don't you go play with your dolls in your room? I'm going to talk to these people for a minute."

"Okay, Mommy!" The little girl took off through the living room and stomped up the staircase at the back of the room.

The woman turned back to us and opened the screen door. "Come on in."

CHAPTER 9

The woman offered us all coffee and stood nervously stirring a ridiculous amount of sugar and cream into her own cup. Andy, Tristan, and I sat at her kitchen table, hands wrapped around steaming mugs and Evie hovered near the pantry door, her eyes watchful. Andy had a notebook and pen out on the table and we could hear Hannah singing upstairs.

She glanced at the ceiling. "She's been singing that song since we moved in." She sat down at the table across from me and placed her palms on the table. She looked tired. "Sorry for all the boxes," she waved a hand at the pile in the corner of the kitchen. "I can't seem to get motivated to get them all emptied out."

"Mrs. Lindemann," I started.

"Call me Kristen."

I nodded. "Well, Kristen, would you like to start by telling us what you've experienced in the house?"

Andy clicked his pen. The sound practically echoed in the quiet kitchen.

Kristen took a deep breath. "Dalton says I'm overreacting. He said that old houses make noises and that I'm stressed from the move and taking care of his mother. She has dementia," she said by way of explanation. Then she dropped her voice. "But, I think something's going on in this house. He doesn't see what I do." She brought her mug to her lips and took a sip.

I noticed the way her hand shook as she put the mug back onto the tabletop. "What do you see?" I asked quietly.

Kristen hesitated. "We moved in a few weeks before Christmas. Dalton drives to St. Joseph to work and sometimes he comes home at night and sometimes he stays overnight there. Anyway, one of the first weeks we were here, I was putting away dishes and Hannah was playing with her favorite doll on the floor over there. That was the first time I heard her sing that song. It sounds like it's in German and I don't know where she picked it up, but she was playing, and all of a sudden I realized she wasn't there anymore. I searched the entire house and thought I saw her upstairs in her room, but then I heard her singing downstairs in the basement." She waved a hand toward the door in the pantry.

Andy scrawled in his notebook, looking up to note the location of the basement while she talked.

"I went down there but all the lights were off. I finally found her digging in a back corner. Her, um, her fingers were bloody from digging at the dirt. I brought her upstairs, washed her up, and bandaged her hands. Dalton went downstairs to look at the basement where she was digging and said he didn't find anything. He put a lock on the door that night and we thought everything was fine. But, the next day, when he left, Hannah kept going to the basement door saying that her friend was down there and she wanted to go play with her." Kristen paused a moment and looked at our faces. Worry creased her features.

"I know," I said quietly. "I do. And, we believe you."

Kristen nodded and went on. "Well, I was fixing lunch and when I went to look for Hannah so she could eat, I found the basement door open. The lock was completely ripped from the doorframe. I ran downstairs and found Hannah in that same spot. She was digging. The, um, bandages were ripped off and her little fingers were bleeding again. This time, though, I saw what she was digging for. In the dirt, buried up to its head was an old doll. To be honest, it really shook me."

"What did the doll look like?" Tristan asked.

"Like one of those antique dolls you see in old photos. It had a porcelain face and these painted glass eyes. The hair was pretty tangled and it was so dirty, but Hannah was absolutely enamored by it, so I got a garden trowel and dug it up the rest of the way for her. We took it upstairs and spent the afternoon cleaning it up, you know, washing its little dress and wiping away most of the dirt. By the time we finished, it looked almost good as new. I mean, it had cracks in the face and the hair probably won't ever look the same as it once did, but Hannah was so happy with her. She named her Toyful, and has been carrying it around now for weeks. She just loves that doll." A smile played across Kristen's mouth, but was replaced by a nervous tight line as she pressed her lips together. She took a sip of coffee, her eyes darting to the ceiling as she did so.

She's hiding something.

"Toyful?" I asked.

Tristan pulled out his phone and started typing.

Kristen smiled. "She comes up with strange names for her dolls all the time. She called one Fruit Snacks for days before we finally settled on Katy."

"Why wouldn't you let her take the doll with her yesterday?" I tilted my head.

Kristen looked up at me.

"I'm sorry. I came by to make sure I was at the right house. I saw you and Hannah leaving and you took the doll and left it on the porch."

"Her grandma doesn't like it." She took another sip of coffee and then looked at me. "I know it sounds crazy, but the last time Hannah took it with her to her grandma's house, my mother-in-law yelled that she didn't want it in the house. She spent the entire visit praying to herself and she didn't calm down until I put Hannah and the doll into the car."

Tristan moved his phone so I could see the screen. The word *teufel* was on his screen and was translated from German to English. I sucked in a breath at the translation: *devil*.

Shaken, I tried to clear my head. "Um, can you show us where you found the doll?"

Kristen's eyes swung up to the ceiling again.

"I'll stay here in case Hannah comes down," Tristan offered.

Kristen took a deep breath. "Let me get the key." She got up and rummaged through a drawer near the stove. Pulling a shiny brass key out of the drawer, she walked to the pantry with it held out in front of her.

"She's scared to death," Evie commented. "There's a red color surrounding her. It feels like anxiety and fear and…poor thing."

Kristen unlocked the lock. It was positioned below a ragged chunk of doorframe. "That's where the first one was." When the door was unlocked, she swung the basement door forward on its hinges. A lone lightbulb hung over the concrete stairs and the wooden framing of the walls was exposed. She flipped the switch and the light turned on. "It's worked ever since that first time I went down to find Hannah. Hold onto the railing. The steps are steep." Kristen led the way downstairs. I followed with Evie behind me and Andy brought up the rear. He pulled the door closed behind us as he cleared the threshold.

"It's cold down here," I commented when we reached the bottom of the stairs.

Kristen led the way through the first large room. She pulled the chain to another lightbulb as she passed through a doorway into a smaller room to our left.

"Do you know much about the history of the home?" Andy asked from behind me as we squeezed through the narrow passage between the concrete wall and the shelves.

"Not really. The realtor said that it was built in the 1950s and it had been on the market for a few years before we bought it. The previous owners retired and moved to Arizona to be close to their son. I don't know how long they lived here, though."

"Do you have much land?"

"Our lot is narrow but long." Kristen moved into another room and pulled the chain on that light. "It goes as far as the mailbox on one side and the shed on the other, but behind us, it goes back almost a mile. It's mostly woods, though. Dalton wants to clear it out this summer and make a dirt bike track. This used to be the coal room when the house was heated by the furnace." She pointed at a small metal door near the floor joists. "They used to shovel it in through there."

Evie stood beside Kristen, staring into the darkness that lay beyond the doorway.

"Are you okay?" I whispered.

Evie nodded her head. "I thought I saw something."

Kristen went into the next room and turned on the light. "It was right over there," she said, her breath hanging in the air in front of her. The temperature dropped several degrees as we came into the space. Andy noted it in his notebook.

The room was small, about ten feet by ten feet. Three of the walls looked older here, made from stone rather than concrete like the other part of the basement. I pulled my phone out of my pocket and turned on the flashlight app. The bright LED shined into the corner where the floor had been disturbed. There was a small hole dug in the hard-packed dirt and the trowel was sticking out of the earth at a jaunty angle near the hole. I looked around, closing my eyes against the pulling feeling. The walls wavered in my line of vision. I knew I was about to have a vision, but I didn't want to scare Kristen, so I began backpedaling my way through the basement.

Andy looked up at me and nodded his head. "So, Kristen, would it be okay for us to talk to Hannah a little bit and maybe see Toyful?"

Kristen agreed. She seemed to be relieved at the suggestion to leave the basement. We retreated at a much faster pace than we arrived. I kept looking over my shoulder as I walked, expecting to see something watching me from the dark corners. The basement definitely had a creepy feeling and I needed to get out of there before I lost myself.

"We need to go back down there, don't we?" Andy asked me while Kristen locked the door again.

I nodded. "Not right now, though."

"How's Evie doing?" he asked.

I glanced at my friend. She looked worried, and tired. "Fine." Under my breath, I said to Evie, "Take it easy. Don't drain all of your energy."

She nodded, her brow knit together. "Let's go upstairs."

"You ready?" I asked Kristen.

"Yeah, come on." She took us through the living room and up the stairs. They creaked under our feet. At the landing, she knocked on the door to her right. The singing from inside stopped. Kristen opened the door. "Hannah, they wanted to see your room."

Hannah squealed and ran to the door. "Hi!"

"Hi, Hannah," I said. "Do you want to show us your new doll? Toyful?"

She shook her head and crossed her arms over her chest.

"What's wrong?" Kristen asked.

"Toyful's been bad," Hannah said.

"Oh, what'd she do?" Kristen smiled.

"She's hiding. I told her not to, but she said you'd be mad."

"Why would I be mad, honey?"

"Because it was your favorite." Hannah held out a hand. Inside was a twisted piece of yellow metal.

Kristen gently took the metal from her daughter's hand. She looked it over and then realization passed over her face and she dropped it to the floor with a clang.

"What is it?" I asked, my stomach tightening.

"It was an angel Dalton made for me out of the brass doorknob from my childhood home. It was a Christmas present from him the first year we were married." She stood looking down at it.

Andy reached down and picked it up. "It's solid brass," he said quietly, turning the twisted metal over and over. It looked like the angel had been crushed into a ball.

"She's sorry, Mommy! She didn't mean to do it."

"Where is Toyful?" I asked.

Hannah turned her wide eyes to me. She shook her head.

"It's okay, Hannah. Tell Marissa where she is."

Evie stepped into the room. "Will you show me?"

Hannah turned to Evie. "I like your hair. It's pretty." She reached up and took Evie's hand.

Kristen's hand flew up to her mouth as she watched her daughter. I insinuated myself near the little girl and Evie so it looked like she might be leading me instead. Hannah led us to her closet and opened the door. She pushed her clothes to the side and got down on her hands and knees. Evie and I did the same and followed her into the small space behind the clothes.

"Scared?" Evie said out of the side of her mouth.

I nodded. "You?"

"I'll be fine."

Hannah disappeared into a small doorway near the corner of the closet. I followed her and put my head into the small space. It was exposed wood, a right angle on one side between the floor and the wall on the back side of the closet. The other wall went from the ceiling of the closet to the floor. A triangle spread out about six feet along the backside of the closet. The cord to a lamp wound around from the outlet behind me to a lamp with an ornate base and a shade with baubles hanging from its edge. Evie moved past me and sat down on the opposite side of the small room. She looked from me to the lamp meaningfully. "It's the one you drew," she said.

I nodded again, and then I looked around at the space. "Where's your doll?"

Hannah sat down on her pallet with a pout. "She's not here anymore."

"Where did she go?" I asked, goosebumps breaking out along my arms as I knelt, my body in the closet and my head in the hidden room.

Hannah shrugged. "I dunno. She'll be back at night-night time."

I furrowed my brow. "She comes at night?"

"Mmmm hmmm. Sometimes Mommy takes her." Hannah pouted, her lower lip shoved out and an angry look on her face.

"She does? Where does she take Toyful?" I asked.

"Read to me!" Hannah handed me a large book and stuck her thumb in her mouth, her wide eyes looking at me expectantly.

"Um, I can't right now. I need to talk to your mommy."

"Move over, squirt," Evie said, settling herself down next to Hannah on the pallet. "I'll read to you."

Hannah squealed with delight.

"Thanks," I mumbled and started to back my way out of the space. I stopped suddenly and stuck my head back in. "Hey, how come she can see you?" I asked.

"Children are more open," was her response.

I decided to ask Tristan about that as I made my way out of the closet and back into the room. Standing up, I brushed my knees. "Toyful's not there," I said.

Kristen bit her bottom lip. "She'll be here tonight."

Cocking my head, I looked at her. "That's the same thing Hannah just said."

"Hannah, honey, we're going to go back downstairs. Come on down and have a snack!" Kristen called.

"Sure, Mommy, when the book is over!" came the response from the closet.

Kristen motioned for us to follow her out of the room. She closed the door gently behind her then turned to us. "She lost the doll a few days before Christmas while she was out playing in the snow. She was absolutely inconsolable. Dalton and I looked all over the property and when we couldn't find it, we told Hannah that we would replace the doll the next day when we could go into town. We went to bed that night, and when we got up in the morning, I went to check on Hannah before making breakfast. When I walked into her room, she was fast asleep, and Toyful was wrapped in her arms."

"Do you think she forgot that she left it in the house?" Tristan offered as he followed Kristen down the stairs.

She shook her head. "That's what we thought until it happened again. It seems like Toyful goes missing at least once or twice a week." Something passed across her features. "But, she always shows up again by the next morning." Kristen laughed nervously, pulling a bag of baby carrots from the fridge. "There have been times I've questioned my sanity in this house."

Andy looked over his notebook. "Is there anything else you can think of that has happened?"

She stared at him for a long minute before her eyes darted to the side and she started washing the carrots under a steady stream of water in the sink. Her back was to me, but the way she held her shoulders, I could tell she was tense.

"Mrs. Lindemann, um, Kristen. We would like to investigate your house," I said. "We would go around and see if we could find evidence of something paranormal happening."

"What would that prove?" she asked, drying the carrots in a paper towel. She turned and leaned against the counter.

"Well, it would validate your claims and make it feel like you're not so..." Tristan started.

"Crazy?" Kristen cut in.

He shook his head. "I was going to say *alone.*"

"Oh."

"If we find that there is indeed paranormal activity occurring, and if we had the opportunity to come in here and spend some time, we could possibly help the spirit that's here," I said.

"I don't think so," Kristen said. She pulled a plastic plate from the cabinet and placed the carrots on it. "Listen, I appreciate your help, but I don't want to be responsible for one of you kids getting hurt."

"A minute ago," I pressed, "we asked if anything else happened. You didn't answer, but I think something did. I think it scared you a lot and you feel like if you talk about it, it will make it real."

Kristen held my gaze for a moment, her eyes unwavering. Then, she drew herself up straight and her face grew blank. "I don't know what you think you saw, but…"

Just then, Evie came down the stairs and stood in the kitchen doorway. "She saw a ghost. She's not sure, but she did." She leaned against the doorway, her face pale. "It was the same little girl you saw playing in the yard."

I squinted at Evie. She seemed less *here.* In fact, I could see right through her. A moment later, she disappeared completely.

Kristen was ushering us out the door, a kitchen towel slung over her shoulder. "I appreciate you coming by, but we're fine. Or, we will be anyway."

Andy and Tristan stood on the front porch. I stopped for a moment in the doorway. "You saw her. The ghost. She has brown ringlets and she's wearing a long blue dress. It has buttons up the back and she has so many freckles."

Kristen froze. She tilted her head to the side. "How did you know that?"

"She's real, Kristen. I saw her, too, right there," I pointed at the front yard.

She stood at the door for a full minute before shaking her head. "I don't want anyone to get hurt."

"We'll be fine," I said. "My dad knows what we're doing and we've helped others before."

"You have?"

I shifted uncomfortably from one foot to the other. "Actually, this would be the first time we're helping someone that's *here*. What I mean is, we've only helped ghosts before. Not anyone living."

"Oh, that doesn't sound creepy at all," Andy whispered. "She's sure to want our help now."

Tristan elbowed him in the ribs.

"How long do you need?" Kristen asked as Hannah came down the stairs behind her.

"We can come back around seven and stay for a few hours tonight," I offered. "It might be best if you and Hannah go somewhere else for the night."

She chewed on her bottom lip again. "We can stay with my mother-in-law."

"Grammy!" Hannah shouted.

Kristen leaned down and picked up the little girl. She jutted her hip out and rested Hannah on it. "Dalton will be spending the night in St. Joseph tonight."

"Perfect," I smiled. "We'll see you then."

"I hope you kids know what you're getting yourselves into," Kristen said as we turned around and walked down the porch steps.

Me, too, I gulped.

CHAPTER 10

"We need all of our equipment," Andy said when we got back to the truck. "Cameras, audio, EMF detectors." His posture was intense as he leaned over the steering wheel.

"He's in his element," Tristan rolled his eyes. "What about that thing you were working on last week? Before we went to the Weeping Bridge."

"The spirit box? I got the external speaker yesterday and we can try it out tonight."

"What's a spirit box?" I asked.

"It's basically white noise. I'm using an app on my old phone and pumping the noise through the external speaker. The thought is that a ghost can use the static to create messages in order to interact with us."

"Oh," I said.

"You felt something back there, didn't you?" Tristan asked.

"She did," Andy confirmed. "In the basement. You didn't go away, though. How'd you manage that, Anderson?"

I shrugged. "I don't know. I guess I knew that if I went under while I was by Kristen, it would scare her."

"Have you ever been able to control it before?" Tristan asked.

I snorted. "Yeah, it wasn't like I was controlling it, though. In fact, if Andy hadn't gotten me out of the basement when he did, I wouldn't have been able to help it."

"The point is you're getting control of things."

I wish I believed that. I stared out the window as Andy drove, the snow-covered landscape stretching out before me. *How was I able to control my visions?* I tried to remember how it felt to push the darkness and pressure away. It felt like when I used to be overwhelmed by thoughts of my mother's death. I would feel the pressure in the middle of my chest, and if I allowed it, it would overtake my entire being and I would lose myself in the sadness and anger. However, somewhere during the last six months, I learned not to lose myself. I learned how to think about my mom and not be overcome with sadness. Evie was why I was able to do that. With her around, I felt brave and in control. I found, though, that when she wasn't around now, I sort of felt the same way. That thought troubled me and I shook my head, clearing it.

"Marissa?"

Tristan's voice jolted me back to the truck. "Yeah?"

"Andy was asking if you wanted him to drop you off at the hospital or your house."

I considered for a moment. "The hospital, I guess. I'm sure Dad's there. I'll see if he'll come home for a little bit this afternoon."

"What time are we meeting?" Tristan asked.

"Six thirty?"

He nodded. "Yeah, I'm going to do some research on the property, so we're headed to my house."

Andy pulled into the porte-cochère in front of the hospital and they both waved as they drove away. I went through the doors and made my way to the elevator, running over what I would say to Evie when I saw her in her room. The elevator doors slid open on the second floor and I got out. At her door, I hesitated, and braced myself for what would greet me in the room. I prepared for the bruises, the swelling, the tubes and the still form of my best friend. Sighing, I pressed the latch and opened the door.

Dad sat dozing in the chair, his feet propped up on the windowsill, a folder of papers on the tray and his laptop on his legs. His head rolled down on his chest and his breathing was heavy.

I looked around the room, trying to avoid looking at Evie's still form on the bed. *Where was she? She said she came here when she needed to recharge. So, where is she?*

"You must be one of Genevieve's friends from school," a voice said from behind me. I moved to the side and allowed the doctor enough room to enter.

"Um, yes, I'm Marissa. Evie's my best friend. That's my dad," I said, nodding toward Dad, who woke up and was rubbing his eyes.

"What's the word, doc?" he asked, his voice thick with sleep.

The doctor flipped the chart open and looked at the machine in the room. "We are concerned with her O-two levels. The oxygen is getting into her body, but for some reason, the body is not processing it. Her levels have been falling steadily for two days now."

"What does that mean?" Dad stood next to the bed, all evidence of exhaustion gone as he stared at the doctor.

"Well, it means that we are going to try a few things to get those levels up, but if that doesn't work, we need to start talking about our other options."

"Our other options," my dad repeated, running a hand through his graying hair.

That's what the doctors said about Mom. My stomach dropped and my legs lost strength. I reached out with a hand and grasped the back of the chair my dad had been sitting in.

He placed a strong hand on my shoulder. "Do what you need to. Bring her back to us," he said, his voice cracking.

The doctor nodded. "We're doing all we can. There's nothing physically wrong with her, but for some reason, she's not responding to any stimuli."

I glanced around the room, willing Evie's spirit to appear. *Where is she?*

When the doctor left, Dad pulled out his phone.

"Who are you calling?"

"Genevieve's father. He needs to come."

Before it's too late, I read in his eyes.

"I have to go."

"Marissa," Dad said as I darted out of the room. I bypassed the elevator and pounded down the stairs. I didn't stop until I was standing outside, gulping huge breaths of icy air. Tears burned hot behind my eyelids and I collapsed on the bench near the doors, the cold metal freezing my rear end even through the thick layer of jeans.

"What's wrong, St. Louis?"

My head snapped up. Evie stood before me, her arms wrapped around her middle. I stood up, anger taking over. "Where have you been? Seriously, Evie! You told me you came here to recharge!"

"I did. Then I went somewhere else," she whispered.

"Where?"

"With Sam. He makes me feel better."

"Do you even care that your body is up there dying? The doctor says that you're not going to make it, Evie." I stared at her, willing her to understand the severity of the situation. "Your father is coming."

Evie stared at me. "He is?"

"Yeah, Dad's up there setting it up right now." All the fight left me and I felt weak again. I sank down to the bench again and placed my head in my hands. "I want you to get better. I don't think I could handle it if I lost you."

"I'm here, though."

I glared at her. "I don't want *this* Evie. She's like a consolation prize. I want the real Evie. I want to hang out with you and do things with you and…and…" I stopped, the tears dangerously close to falling.

Evie sat down beside me. "I know," she said in a quiet voice. She stared down at her folded hands in her lap. "Sam thinks he knows a way to help me get back to my body."

My head snapped up. "He does?"

"Yeah. I don't know all the details yet, but he says that he thinks he can help."

"Evie, what do you know about him?" My stomach roiled. "I mean, what do you really know about him?"

She smiled. "Like, is he a good ghost or a bad ghost?"

"Shut up. You know what I mean."

"He was alive in the early 1900s."

"He told us that on the Ouija board." I looked at her, willing her to move on with her story.

"He worked as a construction worker when they started construction on the City Hall. He was working one day when he got in an accident on the site and he died there. He was only nineteen."

The messages from the Ouija board flew through my mind. "He told us that he was murdered."

She pursed her lips and wound her hands in her lap. "Yeah, he said that he doesn't think he was really killed in an accident. He thinks someone caused it."

I furrowed my brow. "What do you mean?"

She shook her head. "I don't know, and neither does he. He can't remember exactly what happened and it was reported as an accident in the paper. And, since he doesn't remember, we thought maybe you could, you know…" she faded off, an expectant look in her eyes.

"I feel like I'm your personal crystal ball."

"You don't have to if you don't want to," she sighed. "We thought maybe you would want to help him out."

I rolled my eyes. "Of course, I'll help him find out how he died. When do you want to do this? The sooner the better. And, when is he going to know how to get you back in your body?"

"I don't know. He said he had to go talk to someone."

"Who?"

"He didn't say. All he said was that it was someone who knew more about the curtain than he did."

"The curtain between the worlds? What does that have to do with you getting back in your body?"

"The reason I can see the disturbances in the fabric is because those ghosts are trying to affect the real world. They're reaching out for help. Most of them can't break through the fabric to reach the other side, though. So, they press against it, causing the disturbance."

Realization dawned on me. "You're on one side of the fabric and your body is on the other!"

She nodded, sadness in her features. "Yeah, and I don't know how to break through."

I lowered my voice a notch. "*Can* you break through? Can a spirit break the fabric?"

"Sometimes the curtain becomes less dense. You've always heard how the veil between the spirit and human world is more transparent on Halloween?"

I nodded. "Halloween was two months ago."

"Exactly, so we have to figure out a way to make the fabric transparent ourselves."

"How are you going to do that?"

Evie shrugged. "I don't know. That's what Sam went to find out."

"So, when he gets back, we'll figure out how to get you back in your body and then I'll find out how he died."

"He'll want to find that out first."

I made a face.

"He's been a ghost a long time, St. Louis. He doesn't trust the living."

"Sounds to me like he's holding you hostage."

She shook her head. "He's not like that. He's smart, funny, and sweet."

"You like him."

Evie smiled, the color rushing to her cheeks. "Yeah, I do."

I stood up. "Fine, I'll meet with him and find out how he died and then we'll get you back into your body."

"I don't think it's going to be that easy," she said. She looked up at me.

I cocked my head to the side. "Evie, look at your hands."

She looked down at them as they lay folded in her lap. They were nearly see through.

"What's happening?"

"I don't know. If my body's getting weaker, you'd think I would be getting stronger. The opposite is happening. I feel so weak." She stood up and looked wistfully up at the hospital. "I should go be with my body."

I shivered as the words left her mouth and she walked through the doors.

"We're going to help Hannah tonight!" I called after her. "You have to come, Evie!"

She turned and waved at me through the glass of the doors and then disappeared.

Tears filled my eyes and I turned to walk toward the center of town. *If Sam wouldn't help Evie until I helped him, then I was going to get the ball rolling. Right now. My friend didn't have much time left.*

CHAPTER 11

The wind whipped at my hair as I walked down the sidewalk. The nice weather that followed us through Christmas was releasing its hold back to winter's frigidness as the New Year approached. I walked to the end of the street and turned at the corner, my feet taking me downtown. I passed the post office and the diner Dad and I ate in during our first visit to the town nearly three months ago. I wondered if Jessica was working. She would be serving grilled cheese and French fries, and would be blissfully unaware of the drama taking place a few blocks away in the hospital. I wondered for a minute if she'd visited Evie. *Probably not. She never understood why we were friends. Still, it would be a nice gesture.*

Turning the corner, I saw the City Hall and courthouse rising up in the center of the town square. It sat on a hill, a dozen concrete steps leading up to the front doors. Four white pillars held up the balcony above and the windows on the first floor were mirrored by arched windows along the second floor. It was made of red brick that stood in contrast to the two gigantic evergreen trees that flanked it in the snow. Above the second floor was a triangle and above that was a white painted cupola. The eaves were lined with large glass Christmas bulbs that outlined the building in white connect the dots at night. I stood looking up at the building for a moment, wondering where to start looking for Sam.

I walked up to the front doors and pulled at the large, cold brass handle. The door opened with a protesting squeak from its hinges. Inside, the large black and white tiles alternated, leading along a long hallway with offices located on the sides, the lights hanging above reflecting in the shiny surface. I walked along the hallway, my footfalls echoing in the space. As I reached the middle of the building, the ceiling rose two stories above me, two large staircases wrapping left and right around a central desk and an enormous Christmas tree. A girl that looked like she was barely older than I was sat behind the desk, tapping away on the computer, a bored expression on her face. I walked up to the desk and stood there.

After an awkward minute of silence, the girl finally looked up at me. "Can I help you?" she asked.

I cleared my throat, the sound carrying up to the second floor and into the circular space above. "Yeah, um, I was looking for…" I paused. *I'm looking for the ghost of someone who died when this building was being built. You see, my friend's in a medically induced coma, her spirit is having trouble getting back into her body, and I think this ghost, Sam, can help her.* I stared at her blankly for a moment.

"Yes?" She drew the word out, as if she was talking to a small child.

"Sorry, um, yeah. My dad and I just moved here. He's a lawyer and he has a case coming up here next week, so he's been too busy to come down here himself. Would you be able to tell me where the courtroom is, please?" *Stop talking, Marissa,* I chided myself.

The girl looked at her phone and then up at me. "Come on. It's my lunch break. I'll take you by the courtroom on my way to get lunch."

"Thanks," I said.

I followed her through the hallway behind the staircase. She led the way, her heels clicking on the tile as she walked, texting on her phone the whole time.

That was fine with me. In fact, I was worried that if she did talk to me, I would say something stupid.

She passed a set of double doors and waved a hand at it. "Courtroom's there," she said without stopping. "Have a nice day."

"Thanks," I said to her retreating figure. A sign at the door said that court sessions would take place the next week, after the New Year. I yanked on the door and it opened easily. Inside, the lights were dim and the air smelled old and stale. I stepped inside, the heavy door whispering shut behind me. The walls were wood paneled and wooden pews spread out on either side of a narrow aisle carpeted in a tired blue Berber. There was a large wooden judge's bench in the front, flanked by an American flag on one side and the Missouri flag on the other. The room was quiet; the only sound the steady humming of the heaters that ran along the sides of the room.

Dad had taken me to a couple of trials when I was younger and daycare fell through or mom was working late. I remembered what he looked like, standing at the front of the courtroom, his gray suit perfectly pressed and his glasses glinting in the lights. He practiced business law, which I usually found completely tedious and boring, but when he was speaking at the front of the room, I was amazed by his ability to take control of a room.

I heard footsteps behind me and turned to see who it was. There was no one there. I made my way up to the front of the courtroom and pushed open the doorway to the side of the defense table. Another doorway behind the bench led to the judge's quarters, but this door led to holding cells where people were brought from jail and held until their trial date. Dad only let me go back to the holding cells in the courthouse in Soulard once when I was little. There was no one being held at the time, but it frightened me all the same.

I took a deep breath and headed through the doorway. On the other side of a large room was a Sherriff's Department workspace and behind that was a bank of heavy metal doors. They led into small bare rooms with metal benches lining the walls. Ahead was the door leading to the sally port where they pulled up to drop off and pick up prisoners. I gulped. The entire area felt foreboding and too modern with its sleek surfaces and bright fluorescent lights. I shook my head. *No, I'm looking for an older part of the building. A place where he can hide and feel safe.*

"You lost?" The young sheriff spun around in his chair and faced me.

"Um, no, sorry. I was looking for a restroom and took a wrong turn."

The officer stood up and led me over past the public window and back out into the lobby. "Around the stairs on the other side."

"Thanks," I mumbled as the door closed behind him. I walked over and stood at the bottom of the staircase. Above, there was a large iron chandelier hanging down from four chains that were connected to the second floor ceiling. I started climbing the stairs, moving to the side as a couple dressed in matching blue pantsuits passed me going down. They smiled and nodded in my direction, but didn't stop their conversation. I made my way up the rest of the stairs and stood on the second floor. I explored the hallway that spread out on either side of me. One side led to a dozen or so offices and the other to two smaller mediation rooms. Behind the stairs on this floor were restrooms. I pulled open the big wooden door to the women's and stood looking at the huge mirrors over the sink. *Nothing.*

I went out again and stood in the hallway. A small space around the corner caught my eye. There was another door here. It had a red sign affixed to its front that said "stairs." I pushed down on the handle and was met with resistance. It was locked. *Crap.* Something about this door felt right. It was hidden, off the main part of the building, and I guessed it probably led up to the balcony that circled the interior of the cupola.

During the summer a few years before, my mother took me to the Missouri State Capitol to go on a tour. We did the public tour and then wandered the hallways until we found the office of a state representative that was a brother of one of the women Mom worked with. As she was taking a picture of me standing next to the nameplate, the door to the office opened and an aide walked out. His name was Spencer and he took us to all the private places in the capitol. We got to go onto the floor of the assembly room and I even got to sit where the Speaker of the House sat. Then, he took us up to the third floor where we circled the huge balcony. After that, he led us up about a million stairs to a hidden door. We went backstage and climbed steel see-through stairs until we reached the very top of the cupola. He unlocked a door and we stepped out onto the outdoor balcony, staring out across the entirety of Jefferson City. The Missouri River snaked along, a brown sparkling ribbon cutting along the outskirts of the city.

It stood to reason that this staircase might lead to more hidden parts of the building, too. I leaned back and looked down the hallway. When I didn't see anyone on the floor, I pressed up against the door and spoke into the crack, hoping that no one decided to use the restroom while I was speaking. "Sam? My name is Marissa and I'm a friend of Evie's. She told me that you want to figure out how you died. Sam, I can help you." I took a step back and watched the doorway for any sign of movement. *Nothing again.* I leaned back to the open space between the door and its frame. "Listen, Sam, I'm going to hang out here for a while. If you feel like talking to me, I'll be here."

I backed up and slid down until I was sitting in the small space, my back against the cold wall and my feet pressed against the other wall. I closed my eyes and leaned my head back. Something inside me shifted and I allowed it. I allowed the shift to overtake me, pressing down on my shoulders in a familiar way. When I opened them, I was still sitting in the same space, but something was different.

I peeked out around the corner and gasped. Past the restrooms was an open space with scaffolding lining the walls and floors. The space above me was open and I could see the sky through the cupola. Looking down, I realized that I could see nothing but open air below me. Crying out, I scrambled to my feet and grabbed onto the scaffolding behind me for balance. Except, I didn't feel scaffolding beneath my hands. I felt only the smooth surface of the wall. Shaking my head, I stood on a floor that wasn't there. I could see all the way down to the first floor as it was being built. *My mind is here, but my body is still in the real world.* The realization hit me full force. I decided I would have to be careful not to move around while I was in this vision. What would people think of a girl walking around, bumping into things she could feel but couldn't see?

I stood there, looking around me. Workers milled around the area like ants. Most wore white shirts rolled up at the sleeves and newsboy hats. Some had mustaches and some wore suspenders. Horses and carriages were visible through the half-constructed walls and women in long dresses walked along the sidewalks. I felt like a time traveler. Behind me, a young man worked on the scaffolding, laying brick alongside an older man with gray in his mustache. The young man whistled as he spread mortar along the top of a brick and placed a new brick on the top, pushing it down until the mortar squeezed out the sides. He swept the overflow away with a trowel and laid down another layer on the next brick. He looked up as the scaffolding swung with the movement of the older man.

"Careful, Manny."

The older man laughed and clapped the younger man on the back. "You must be part chicken."

"I ain't a chicken. Just don't like heights," the young man mumbled. He went back to his work, his brown eyes intent on the job at hand.

Sam? Is that you?

The young man looked up for a moment, the wind tossing the brown curls that snuck out under his newsboy cap.

"Aye. It's me," a voice said behind me.

I spun around and came face to face with a second version of the young man on the scaffolding. The floor was again visible and the walls were finished, enclosing me in the small space.

Sam stood before me, his hands shoved deep in his pockets.

"How did you see that?"

"Evie told me you were special," he replied.

"But no one has ever been able to see what I see before."

Footsteps echoed in the hallway behind us.

"Come on," he said, beckoning me through the open door. I looked behind me once more and followed Sam through the door to the stairs beyond.

CHAPTER 12

The stairs were poorly lit and cobwebs clung to the corners where the walls met the ceiling. At the top, the corridor took a sharp left and led to another door. He opened this one as well and we climbed two more flights of stairs into the attic space of the old building.

Up here, the trusses and wood of the roof offered little barrier to the cold winter outside. I could see my breath as we climbed and drew my coat closer around my shoulders. At the top of these stairs, a door led to the balcony. Sam passed this and wound his way around wooden beams. The only light up here came through the circular window. I took a quick inventory of where we were in the building and decided that we were near the triangular place above the second floor. Under the window, a quiet alcove provided a place to see out the window. Sam motioned for me to take a look and I leaned forward, my breath immediately fogging the window. I smiled and used my sleeve to wipe away the moisture.

The City Hall sat almost exactly in the middle of Culvers Grove and as I looked out the window, I could see the streets leading into the town square like spokes of a giant wheel. The snow was beginning to fall and it clung to the branches of the trees below. I turned to Sam, who was sitting with his back resting against a wooden beam.

"Is this where you," I hesitated and changed the word quickly before it left my mouth, "stay?"

He nodded.

"Is this where Evie visits you?"

He nodded again.

"Can you leave this place?"

This time, he shook his head, a note of sadness in the motion.

I sat quietly for a moment. "She's dying. Evie's body is dying."

Sam turned his brown eyes to me. They were deep and pensive. "I know. I'm trying to help her."

"Why?"

He looked surprised by my question but recovered quickly. "I care about her. I met Genevieve when she reached out to me. I was able to talk to her through a spirit board. She contacted me and we spoke together many times. Then, when she had her accident, I was able to contact her directly."

I raised my eyebrow. "You're able to contact other ghosts?"

He furrowed his brow. "No, I only meant that instead of talking to her, I actually was able to see her. Touch her." His face took on a wistful quality. "She came to find me."

I sat down across from him, my breath hanging in the air as I thought of what to ask next, my questions spinning through my head. Every question led to about ten more and I tried to organize them. "First of all, do you know how to get her back into her body?"

"Not as of yet. I have to meet with someone that knows much more than I do about this place."

"And, when you say 'this place,' you're referring to the ghost world?"

"Yes."

"How do you contact him if you have to stay here?"

"He's here, too?"

I sighed. "Who is it?"

Sam folded his hands in his lap and leaned forward. "I don't know his name or even if he has one. He's older than this building, this place, maybe even this town."

"Where is he?"

"I don't think I can tell you."

Anger sparked. "Listen, I'm here to help you so that you can help my friend. But, if you're going to be cagey about things…"

Sam held out his hands. "Please don't get angry." He took off his hat and rubbed his hand through his hair. "I don't know how much I can tell you."

"Fine, I get it. Evie said you don't trust the living."

"I trust *her*."

"You have to help her. She said that you wouldn't help her until I help you figure out how you died."

Sam looked like I hit him in the face. He stood up and began pacing. "I never said such a thing! I told her that I would like to find out how I died, but finding out how to save her is not contingent upon this information."

Evie. Realization dawned. "She told me that so I would help you. She didn't think I would do it unless I thought it would save her." I looked up at Sam. "She's wrong. I want to help. In fact, that's all I want to do. We're going to a house tonight to help a little girl and her family." I shook my head. "I don't know why I'm telling you."

"Because you want me to know that you're a good person and you would help me even if I wasn't helping your friend." He squatted down across from me and dipped his head to catch my gaze. "Right?"

I nodded. "I guess."

"Are you scared?"

"No, um, not really. It's, well, I usually don't do stuff like this without Evie. She's the brave one."

He stood up. "You're braver than you give yourself credit for." Sam walked over and looked out the window. "I am planning to contact the person I need to talk to tonight after the living have left the building."

"That leaves us a couple hours. Let me text my dad and then I'll see if I can see how you died."

Sam chuckled. "You're different, aren't you?"

I bristled. "What do you mean?" I asked, my thumb poised over the keyboard on my phone.

He laughed. "I meant no disrespect. I only meant that I see a lot of people your age come through here and you're not like any of them."

"You're not that much older than me," I mumbled.

"I was nineteen when I died, but I have been around since 1904." He tipped his hat to me. "I've seen a lot."

I texted my dad and hit send, letting him know that I was at Andy's house and he would bring me home later. Then, I placed my phone back in my pocket and stood up. "How do we do this?"

"Geez, St. Louis, aren't you like an expert at this by now?"

"Genevieve!" Sam's face lit up.

"Hey, there," she said, walking over and wrapping him in a hug.

He leaned down and kissed the top of her head. Something stung inside as I watched. *Grant holds me the same way when we're together.* I shook the thought from my head.

"What are you doing here?" I asked.

"I checked the normal places, and when you weren't there, I figured you'd be here. I'm glad you two finally met." Evie's face was flushed and her black curls swirled around her face in an ethereal manner. She clung to Sam's hand as she talked to me.

"We're going to show Sam how he died."

"I think Manny pushed him from the scaffolding."

Sam shook his head. "I don't know. That's the problem. I remember working here and I remember being on the scaffolding, but I don't remember anything after that. Except darkness. Darkness for a long time." A shadow passed across his face.

Evie squeezed his hand. "She'll find out. I promise." Her gaze turned to me and I could see the pleading in her eyes. This was really important to her.

And, if it was important to her, it was important to me.

"Okay," I said, "I'm going to sit here and close my eyes. If this is where you died, I should be able to see what happened."

I sat down and crossed my legs. Sam and Evie sat down across from me and watched me expectantly.

The pressure built and my ears popped. "Something's happening," I mumbled. I closed my eyes and let the feeling wash over me. When I opened my eyes, we were again sitting on open air. The wooden beams and trusses created a skeletal pattern in the moonlight. "It's nighttime," I said. "No one's here. No, wait," I said, watching as a figure crossed the large town square and made his way to the construction site. "Is that you?" I squinted, trying to see through the thick blanket of darkness to the yard almost three stories below. The figure paused and then darted up the steps into the building. When he got inside, he closed the doors behind him and took his hat off, running his hand through his hair.

I watched as he walked along the main floor. "What are you doing? Why are you here after dark?" I asked.

"I don't remember this," Sam whispered from next to me.

"You can see this, too?" I glanced over.

Sam nodded, his eyes intent on his figure below. "It's all I can see."

"What?" came Evie's voice. "What can he see?"

"Shhh, I can see what she's seeing," Sam responded.

Sam's figure looked around and then walked to a doorway along the back wall.

"Where are you going?" I asked, as the figure disappeared beyond the door.

"We need to go down there," he said, standing up.

"I can't," I said. "Not while there are people here."

Evie stood up. "I can lead you both downstairs. I can't see what you do, so I'll be able to get you downstairs."

"You can't touch me," I reminded her.

"Fine, I'll just have to give you directions."

I glanced over at Sam, his image superimposed onto the vision of the past.

"St. Louis?"

I nodded. "Lead the way." I watched as Evie started toward the stairs that I couldn't see. "Stay close," I told Sam.

We made our way down the first set of stairs, my feet treading above empty air as I followed. This was like the most intense game of Trust I had ever played and my heart was in my throat the entire time. Evie opened a door and then another at the bottom of the stairs. She looked out first and then motioned us to follow. I could feel my energy draining and wasn't sure how much more of this I could take.

Evie led us through the second floor to the circular staircase. We made our way down and then followed her through the hallway to the door where the figure disappeared. Down there, the construction was almost complete, so my feet were on solid ground again. It didn't make me feel any better. Since hitting this floor, wave after wave of nausea hit me and I bit my bottom lip against the sick feeling rising in my chest. The floors and walls seemed to vibrate and I felt lightheaded.

"What's wrong?" Evie asked.

"Nothing." I tried to smile but the feeling of sickness was overwhelming my senses and I was getting weaker as the moments ticked on.

"It's locked," Evie whispered to Sam.

He nodded and reached out to touch the door. It fell open at his touch and swung out to reveal the first three steps of a staircase leading down to a solid block of concrete.

As soon as the door opened, a piercing pain railed at my head. My hands flew up and I grasped both sides of my head, trying to stop my head from literally splitting apart. The air felt heavy and thick and it became hard to breathe. I sucked in a wheezing breath, trying to bite back the bile that was filling my throat.

"They filled it in," Sam whispered. "My God, they filled it all in."

"Hey, you can't be down here!" A voice caused me to spin around. A security guard was striding toward me. "That area is off limits!"

"Sorry," I squeaked out as I tore past him, my hand over my mouth. The vision disappeared around the edges and I was back to reality, but the sick feeling didn't dissipate at all. In fact, it got worse as all my senses were assaulted at once. I barely made it out the door before I bent over, retching into a trashcan near the double doors. A man standing on the porch talking on his phone turned to glare at me as he covered the mouthpiece on his phone.

"Sorry," I mumbled, wiping at my mouth with the back of my hand.

"What the heck happened back there?" Evie said, breathless as she caught up with me.

"I don't know, Evie, but I have to get out of here." I stumbled down the steps to the sidewalk below.

Evie followed, turning to wave at Sam, who was standing in the doorway, his hands shoved into his pockets as he watched us walk away.

"What did you see? What happened?" she asked.

"Andy's..." I managed to say. All of my concentration was on staying upright, putting one foot in front of the other.

We walked the three blocks to his house and knocked on the door. His mom answered the door and took one look at me before ushering me into the house. "My goodness, you look terrible. Should I call your dad?"

"Maybe Andy could give me a ride home?"

"Andy," she called from the living room, "come take your friend home!"

"I'm sorry, Mrs. Bryant," I said as I sat down on the couch.

Andy came into the room, took one look at me, and grabbed his keys. "I'll be back tomorrow morning, Mom." He gave her a peck on the cheek as he passed.

I was grateful for his arm as he placed it around me and helped me to his truck. Evie was already in the bed of the truck, worry creasing her features.

Andy smiled. "I assume you're going to fall asleep in the truck and keep me in suspense until you've had your beauty rest, huh?"

I shot him a glare as he hoisted me into the passenger seat of his truck. He closed the door behind me.

I was asleep before he climbed in and started the truck.

CHAPTER 13

I woke up in my own bed, the comforter pulled up to my chin. The television was on and Andy and Tristan sat together on my futon, watching an old Laurel and Hardy movie. Evie perched on the dresser, her eyes never leaving me as I sat up and rubbed a hand over my face.

"It's a party, huh?" I asked.

"I didn't think you'd mind if I picked up Tristan on the way over. It wasn't like you were a great conversationalist." Andy smiled.

I drew my knees up to my chest. "Sorry about that. What time is it?"

"Around three," Andy said, standing up to stretch.

"What were you doing?" Tristan leaned around Andy to look at me. "Were you seeing something?"

I explained about Evie and Sam, and about what we saw.

"What was he doing there after dark?" Tristan asked.

"Pretty shady, if you ask me," Andy quipped.

Tristan gave him a severe look. "Evie's here, I think."

"She is," I nodded toward the dresser.

"Sorry, Patton."

Evie hopped down from the dresser and paced the floor. "He's going to talk to the person he needs to talk to tonight. To try to find out how to get me back into my body."

"Do you know who it is?"

Evie stopped and shook her head. "He only said that it's an old spirit. One he's heard about but has never met. He seemed pretty nervous about going to talk to him." She bit at her thumbnail.

"He'll be safe," I said, trying to send out waves of encouragement to her.

"What happened to you?" she asked.

I translated for the boys and then sat on my bed quietly for a moment. "I don't know what happened. As soon as that door opened, I felt like I was dying. Seriously, I've never felt that way before." *I was lying.*

"Yes, you have," Evie challenged. "You felt like that at the bridge the first time."

"I remember."

"And, you felt that way when your mom died."

I rested my chin on my knees. "Yeah, I did."

"What do you think was down there?" Andy asked.

Tristan already had his phone out, typing madly at the keyboard. A moment later, he looked up. "Listen to this. I found an article about the courthouse from the 1990s."

"Read it."

"It was written in May 1994. It says that the courthouse was the scene of a tragic death in the early nineties. A city councilwoman's daughter was visiting the courthouse on a school trip. Her teacher couldn't find her when it was time for lunch and when they went to look for her, they found that she had fallen into a well in the basement. She was dead by the time they were able to pull her from the water. After that, there were several incidents reported of strange things happening at the courthouse. Doors slamming shut, people getting ill, shadows lurking around corners. Anyway, the councilwoman petitioned the city to fill in the well and the city council approved a plan to block off the entrance to the basement. They built a structure around the stairs to the basement and filled it with concrete."

"Seems like overkill," Andy said. "I mean, couldn't they have filled in the well or gotten a big lock for the door?"

"It says here that the councilwoman felt that permanently barring the entrance was the right thing to do."

"Does it say if the activity stopped?" I asked.

"It says that immediately after blocking the entrance, all activity stopped."

"That sounds like a ghost story, not a real thing that happened."

Tristan shrugged. "Maybe the city councilwoman heard the ghost stories about Sam."

Evie perked up. "What ghost stories?"

Tristan slid his finger across his screen. "During construction of the building, there were two deaths. One was a man named Carter Jefferson. The cause of death was listed as an accident due to falling debris. The other was a Samuel Johnson."

Evie took a sharp breath in.

"What was the cause of death?" I asked.

"Doesn't say. Listed as an accident but no details."

"That's your Sam," I said.

Evie nodded.

"I need to get into the basement if I want to see what happened to him," I said. "But, I don't think I can. Are there any other entrances?"

Tristan shook his head. "I don't think so. The basement was used for holding cells at the beginning. So, there wouldn't have been multiple entrances."

"One way in, one way out," Andy said. "You got anything to eat, Anderson?"

"Um, yeah. I'm hungry, too. I think there's a frozen pizza or two in the freezer." I threw the cover off and swung my legs off the bed.

"Two's good." Andy got up from the futon.

I looked at Evie's face. "You guys go throw them in. I'm going to talk to Evie for a minute."

They left the room and I turned to Evie. "What are you thinking?"

She nodded. "I think I should go down to the basement."

"You can get down there?"

She nodded again. "Yeah, Sam showed me how and I've been practicing. She walked toward my closet door and passed right through it, then came back out again. "I wasn't able to do that at first, but the longer I'm, well, like I am, the more things I can do."

"That's not a good thing," I said, my stomach clenching uncomfortably. "That means your body is getting weaker, I think."

"I know, but listen, I think I can get to the basement."

I shook my head. "I don't think that sounds like a good idea at all. What are you going to accomplish by being there?"

"Maybe I can find another way in."

"Fine, but not tonight. We have to go help Kristen and Hannah. I'm going to need you there."

"You don't need me." Evie stood staring out the window. "You're going to have to be okay without me if Sam can't figure out how to get me back in my body."

I stood there, letting the enormity of what she was saying sink in. It felt like my insides were on fire and I closed my eyes. "We're going to figure this out and get you back to your normal self."

She turned and faced me. "I sure hope you're right, St. Louis."

I walked downstairs with her and met the boys in the kitchen. Tristan sat on the counter while Andy got the frozen pizzas ready to put in the oven. He added extra mozzarella cheese and mushrooms to the top of one and some crumbled leftover taco meat on the other.

"Did you have a chance to find out anything about the house we're investigating?" I asked, pulling a chair out and sitting down in it backwards.

"I was able to find out a few things." Tristan jumped down from the counter and came to sit next to me at the table. "So, the original house was built in 1848 by the son of German immigrants, Joseph Schmidt. He married

Bethany and they had a son, Hans, and a little girl, Amalie." He pulled out his phone and scrolled through a couple of screens. In 1856, the original house burned down, leaving only the foundation and the small cellar behind. Both of the children perished in the fire but they never found the little girl's body. In 1947, Louis and Winifred Kennison bought the property and built the house we are going to on the old site. They added a partial basement to the existing cellar and then put up a two-story house over that. They lived there until they moved away a few years back and then Kristen and her husband bought the property."

Something nagged at my memory. "Say those names again, the ones who built the house."

Tristan cocked his head to the side. "Joseph and Bethany Schmidt."

Where had I heard those names before? I watched as Evie claimed a spot on the counter and sat down. Andy checked the pizzas.

"Has the cheese even melted yet?" I teased.

"I'm so hungry I don't even care if I chip a tooth on the crust."

"Your mom will care after she spent so much money on your braces," Tristan said.

The sound of Andy opening the oven again made me smile. Then, like a lightning bolt, it hit me. "The cemetery!"

All three of my friends turned to look at me.

"More words would be helpful here," Andy said.

"Sorry, um, do you guys remember the first time we went out to the cemetery together?"

Tristan nodded. "Yeah…"

"Well, I remember where I heard those names before. Evie and I walked over to the oldest part of the cemetery and we saw four gravestones: one for a Joseph Schmidt, one for his wife, Bethany, and then two smaller white crosses."

"I remember that!" Evie hopped down and crossed the kitchen to sit down at the table. "It was right before you heard whispering."

"Right."

"That's the family then, but there were different dates on the headstones." I tried to recall the dates, but couldn't seem to pull them up. And, I couldn't remember seeing dates on the crosses at all. "Did you find out where the family went after the fire?"

"They moved to Bethany's sister's house in town and lived there the rest of their lives. Bethany's sister had three children and a great-great niece of hers still lives here. You know the green house on Walnut?" he asked Andy.

Andy nodded and turned his attention back to the oven.

"I want to head down to the basement first thing." I leaned my chin on my arms that were crossed over the back of the chair.

"I have all of the equipment. Tristan helped me load up the truck earlier." Andy checked the pizzas again. "They're done."

The kitchen filled with the warm smell of melted cheese. My stomach growled and I realized I hadn't eaten anything except cereal this morning. I stood up and grabbed three plates from the cabinets. When I heard the crunch of gravel outside, I opened the cabinet and pulled one more plate out.

Andy cut the pizza and was divvying out slices when Dad walked through the back door.

"Just a quick stop," he said, grabbing a plate as he walked to the table. "I have to be back at the hospital by five-thirty. Hey, Andy. Tristan."

"What's going on?" I asked, scooping the melted cheese that oozed across my plate back onto my slice of pizza.

"Genevieve's mother is getting off work early to come see her."

Movement stopped in the kitchen and everyone stared silently at my dad. I glanced over at Evie. She pressed her lips together.

"Does that mean she helped you get in touch with her dad?" I asked, finally.

Dad looked around the kitchen. "Is she…*here*?"

I nodded. "Yeah, she's sitting right there." I indicated the chair at the far end of the table.

"Hello, Genevieve. I want you to know that I was able to contact your father this afternoon. He's made plans to hop the next plane to Missouri and I'm driving to pick him up in Kirksville tomorrow morning." He sat quietly for a moment. "Do you have any questions, Genevieve?"

I turned to look at Evie. She was absolutely still, her expression unreadable.

"Do you have any questions?" I repeated.

She blinked and looked at me as if she was surprised that I was there. "Oh, um, I guess I want to know where he was, and why he left. Why he left me with *her*. I want to know what he was so afraid of that he left me."

I cleared my throat. "She, um, she wants to know where he lives."

"That's the interesting thing. He's been living in Austin all of these years. He's an electrician and works with a large construction company there. He's never remarried and he doesn't have any other kids."

"She also, um…" I glanced up at her again. Her face was unmoving. "Wants to know why he left her mother and her."

Dad pushed his plate away and laced his fingers on the table. He stared right at the empty chair where Evie was sitting. "Genevieve, I don't know the story, but I am prepared to hear what he has to say about the matter. I also want you to know that this doesn't change anything. Marissa and I still want you to be part of this family."

Evie nodded. "Tell him thanks."

"She says thank you."

Dad didn't move for a moment. "Genevieve, if you would like, I'd be happy to take you with me to the hospital when your mother is there. It's completely up to you, but I wanted to extend the offer. She held up her part of the deal, so I'm going to get her in to see you."

Evie put her head down and stared at her hands.

"Does she want to come?" Dad whispered to me.

I shrugged. "Evie, what do you want to do?"

"I feel like I should go, but I'm scared."

"Of what?"

Evie's eyes filled with tears. "I'm scared that she'll be the mom I remember and loved. I'm scared that I'm hurting her and I don't want to do that."

"I'll go with you," I said. "I'll be brave for you, Evie."

She looked up at me. "You're such a sap, St. Louis." Her smile let me know my answer.

"She'll go, but she wants me to come, too. And, she doesn't want her mom to know that she's a, you know, ghost."

"I understand. Then, it's settled. We'll head to the hospital after this, and Andy and Tristan can meet you there." He pulled his plate back and tucked in, the cheese making a trail from his mouth to the slice of pizza.

CHAPTER 14

The ride to the hospital was quiet. Dad listened to talk radio the whole way and I kept glancing back to the bed of the pickup to make sure she hadn't changed her mind and bailed. Evie said she didn't want to chance coming into contact with me, and since she didn't get cold anymore, she opted for the bed of the pickup.

"Are you scared?" Dad asked, reaching over to turn down the volume.

"Of what? You'll have to be more specific," I said. "Really, it's usually a very long list."

He chuckled. "Of going out to investigate tonight?"

I rolled it around in my mind for a minute. "Not really, I think we're looking for a little girl ghost."

"How are you going to help her?"

I shrugged. "I don't know yet. We're planning to stay a few hours tonight."

Dad nodded and pulled a butterscotch from his shirt pocket. "Well, you know I have to tell you to be careful."

"I will. Andy, Tristan, Evie and I will be there. The house will be locked and we'll all have phones on us. I'll text you the address and home phone number if you need anything."

Dad was quiet for a moment. "Do you think Genevieve's mother is going to show?"

I whipped my head around to look at him. The thought hadn't even occurred to me and then I chided myself for being so naïve. "I don't know."

"Do you think she's going to be okay if she doesn't?"

I turned around to look at Evie. She was sitting in the back of the truck, staring at the setting sun as Dad drove into town. "I think she'll be surprised if she *does* show up."

A little later, Dad went down to wait by the back door of the hospital. I stayed in the room with Evie.

"Do you think she's going to show up?" She stared down at her lifeless body lying in the bed.

"I don't know, but if she doesn't, we're still here for you. And your dad will be here tomorrow morning."

"Quit worrying, St. Louis. It wouldn't be like it was the first time she's disappointed me."

At that moment, the door to the room opened and Dad held it open for Evie's mom. He ushered her in and she stood at the foot of the bed. Her hand flew to her mouth and her eyes filled with tears. She shook her head back and forth, "Baby girl," she muttered over and over again. "Oh, my baby girl."

Evie stood on the side of the bed, her arms crossed over her chest. "Look at her eyes, St. Louis. How can she already be drunk? She got off work, like, twelve seconds ago!"

I squinted and looked at Evie's mom. She barely glanced in my direction as she moved around the bed, stumbling a bit as she did so. Dad came over to stand by me.

"She's drunk," I whispered.

"I know," he said, his eyes watchful as Tammy leaned over Evie's sleeping form and ran a hand down her cheek. "Her boyfriend is waiting in the car downstairs. Three beer cans rolled out of the car when she got out."

I felt anger well up inside me. *How could she show up drunk to see her daughter?*

"Calm down, St. Louis." Evie said from across the room.

I looked up at her questioningly.

"Oh, get off it. I can see the color rolling off you. You look like you're boiling." She looked at her mother. "She's sad. Really sad, but there's something else there, St. Louis." She tilted her head to the side. "She's afraid, too. The fear is muted, but it's there. There's also…"

I peered at Evie's mom, trying to discern her mood. All I could see was a drunk woman with watery eyes and bad skin. The woman who had beaten my best friend. I felt my stomach clench.

"…decay."

My eyes snapped up and I looked at Evie.

She met my gaze. "Ask her if she's okay?"

I cleared my throat. "Um, Ms. Patton?"

Evie's mom looked up at me, her eyes bloodshot and deep set. "I have nothing to say to you," she growled. She leaned over the still form of her daughter and glared at me. When she spoke again, her lips pulled back from her yellow teeth. She reminded me of a wild animal. "You moved to this town and took my baby girl away from me. You did this to her!" she yelled.

Dad took a step closer to me. "Ms. Patton, I'm going to have to ask you to keep this civil. I got you in to see Genevieve, but please remember that there is still a protective order in place."

"You bet there is!" she growled, turning her fury in my dad's direction. "And, I'm going to the courts tomorrow to tell them that you broke the order!"

Dad took a deep breath. "This is not how this is going to work, Ms. Patton." He pulled a form from the folder on the chair. "I filed a temporary order of visitation for you today." He handed her the letter. "You're allowed to see her this one time."

Evie's mother took the paper and read over it. "You think of everything, don't you?" Her eyes flashed up.

"I think only of what is best for my family."

"She's not your family!" she shouted.

"Not yet," Dad said. He reached over and placed his thumb on the call button. "Now, you can remain civil and talk to your daughter, or you can be escorted out of here. Your choice." His voice was ambivalent, but his eyes were watchful and protective.

Evie's mother pulled her purse strap up on her bony shoulder and stood up straight. "Fine, I have to go anyway." She looked back down at Evie. "Hope you make it through this, kid, but if you don't, Bob and I are going to Cabo on your life insurance." With that, she turned on her heel and walked out the door my dad held open for her.

He met my eyes. "I'm going to make sure she gets out of the building. Stay with her?" He nodded his head toward Evie.

"Sure," I managed around the lump in my throat.

The door closed and Evie and I were left alone. I waited for Evie to say something witty to brush away her mother's comment. It never came. Instead, Evie sat down on the chair, put her head down on her knees and sobbed.

I walked around the bed and stood helplessly by her side, wishing more than anything that I could hug her, give her some comfort. "Oh, Evie," I whispered, "I'm so sorry."

Dad came back into the room and let the door close behind him. He shook his head. "I never would have had her come if I would have known." He rubbed a hand across his tired eyes. "I'm so sorry, Genevieve."

She continued to cry and I stood there, shifting from foot to foot. "I don't know what to do," I said, splaying my hands in front of me. "She's crying, Dad."

"Genevieve, dear," Dad started.

The room was silent except for the sound of the machines working. I looked over. "She's gone."

"Where did she go?"

"To see Sam."

CHAPTER 15

"You guys ready for this?" Andy asked as I climbed in the truck. "Patton's here, right?"

"Not yet, but she promised she'd come," I said as I closed the door behind me. I glanced up at the hospital. I thought about Dad sitting there by Evie's side and wondered if he would go home tonight. I doubted he would, though. It seemed like he lived and breathed at the hospital lately. I pushed the twinge of jealousness down and then chastised myself for feeling it in the first place. *He's worried about Evie. It doesn't mean he loves you any less.* It didn't quell the feeling that this happened before when my mom was in the hospital.

I tossed around the thought of telling Andy and Tristan about Evie's mom, but I decided to wait until she was here. It didn't feel like my story to tell.

"This is going to be epic," Andy said, turning onto a gravel road.

The rest of the drive, we sat in nervous silence, only breaking it occasionally to check on a procedure and make sure we each knew what we would be doing. We got to Kristen's house around seven and saw her red car parked in the driveway. Dalton's truck was gone. We stepped out into the still, moonlit night and took the things that Andy handed us from the toolbox on the back of his truck. Weighted down with equipment, we trudged up to the front porch.

I rang the doorbell.

A few moments later, Kristen opened the door. I could hear Hannah screaming in the background.

"She can't find her doll," Kristen said by way of explanation as she held the door open for us.

We came in and placed the equipment in a pile by the front door.

Hannah sat on the couch, her face red and tear-streaked.

"You lost Toyful?" I asked.

"Her name's Hilda," Hannah said under her breath.

I glanced up at Kristen and she shrugged.

"Why did you change her name?" I asked.

Hannah sniffed loudly. "The little girl said it was her name." She stuck her lower lip out and it trembled. She took a deep, hitching breath.

"Hey, Hannah," Evie said, walking through the door behind us.

I breathed a sigh of relief as she leaned down to speak to the crying little girl on the couch. "We're here to find your doll, okay?"

Hannah turned red eyes in Evie's direction. I stood directly behind Evie so it looked like she was looking at me. "We'll find Hilda," I said.

"She's gone!" Hannah wailed.

I turned to Kristen. "She didn't come back this morning?"

"She did. When Hannah woke up this morning, the doll was sitting on her nightstand. She played with her all day, and then, as we were packing up to leave, she disappeared again." She dropped her voice. "Probably best since my mother-in-law doesn't like the doll anyway."

Evie sat down next to Hannah on the couch and they started talking.

"Is there anything we need to know before you leave?" I asked.

Kristen thought for a moment. "I'll leave an extra key by the door. If you can, lock up before you leave. I picked up some soda and there's a pizza in the fridge if you get hungry." Kristen looked around the house.

"We're going to figure out what's going on in your home, so hopefully, by the time you get back tomorrow morning, everything will be quiet," I reassured her.

She closed her eyes and sighed. "That would be wonderful. I haven't slept a full night in this house since we moved in." The circles under her eyes told me that she wasn't exaggerating.

I patted her arm, like my mother used to do when I was nervous about something. "It will all be over soon."

"My number's by the fridge. Call me if you need anything."

"We will."

"Hannah, honey, come on. Let's go visit Grammy."

Hannah turned from Evie and looked up at her mom. "The nice lady says they're going to look for Hilda."

"If we find her, we'll put her in your room. Would that be okay?" I asked.

Hannah stuck a pudgy thumb in her mouth and nodded. She reached up for her mom and Kristen picked her up, resting her on a hip while she swung the strap of her overnight bag onto her shoulder. "Call if you need anything," she said again. She hesitated at the door. "Are you sure about this?"

"It will be fine, Kristen," I said. "Have a good night and we'll see you tomorrow. Bye, Hannah."

Hannah waved a hand at Evie and then they slipped out the door. I flipped the lock behind them and we stood in the living room until we heard their car drive away up the road.

"Pizza first?" Andy said.

I shot him a glare.

"Fine, Mom," he joked. "Tristan, you put cameras in Hannah's room. Make sure you have it pointed toward her closet. I need another feed from the room behind her closet, too. Headquarters will be in the kitchen. I'll set the monitors on the table. Then, we'll get the audio set up."

"What should I do?" I asked.

Andy squinted at me.

"And don't give me any of that 'you're our sensitive tonight' stuff either. You're a man down and Evie can come with me to tell me what to do."

He sat for a moment and then seemed to make up his mind. "Fine, you take this camera down to the basement. Set it up in the oldest part and have Evie show you how to angle it toward the corner."

"Got it, boss," I said, slinging the strap of the camera bag over my shoulder. I started toward the pantry.

"You'll need this." Andy waggled the end of an orange extension cord in my direction. "And, take this, too." He handed me a walkie. "Channel twelve. Hold the button down to talk."

I retraced my steps and took the cord from him, carefully threading it behind me while I walked to the pantry again. I turned to make sure Evie was following me. At the door, I took a minute to turn the lock and then flipped the switch to turn on the light over the stairs. Taking a deep breath, I started down the steps, the cord unwinding along behind me.

The basement felt heavy again, foreboding, and I tried to ignore the feeling as it pressed around me. The pressure grew as Evie and I wound our way through the labyrinthine corridors to the back of the basement. Here, I placed the bag on the floor in the middle of the room.

"Do you feel that?" I asked Evie.

She wrapped her arms around her middle and nodded her head. "So, you'll need to set up the tripod here," she motioned to the corner of the room.

I followed her instructions and got the camera attached to the tripod on my second try. Then, I plugged it in and flipped out the viewing pane from the side. "I don't see anything," I noted.

"Lens cap," Evie said.

"Oh." I squeezed the tabs and the lens cap fell to the front, swinging back and forth on the little cord hanging from the camera. The basement came into focus on the small screen. Evie directed me to tilt the camera up and then down, capturing as much of the little room as it could.

"That's good." I heard Andy's voice come through the walkie at my side.

"Looks like we're done," Evie said.

"Hold on." I peered through the viewer. "I see something." In the viewer, there was something moving in the corner." The pressure built and I could feel a vision pressing in on me. "Evie, I'm going to see something."

She shuffled from one foot to the other. "Let Andy know."

I nodded and pressed the button, bringing the walkie to my mouth. "Andy, I see something on the camera down here."

"I don't," he said. Then, "Oh, you're *seeing* something. On my way."

His footsteps came through muffled as I leaned down to look through the camera. In the corner, there was a woman's figure. She was an older woman, very plump, and dressed in a pair of maroon knit pants with the seam up the fronts of the legs. Her shirt had flowers and a collar and her hair was all gray and placed in evenly spaced curls over her head. She held something in her hands.

I looked up from the camera and saw the woman in the corner of the basement. She glanced over her shoulder and then knelt down with a groan, her arthritic knees popping with the motion. When she was on her knees, she began to dig. She used a garden trowel and dug at the hard-packed dirt until she made a hole about a foot across and a couple feet down. Dragging her sleeve across her forehead, she sat back on her haunches for a moment, breathing hard.

"What do you see?" Andy's voice was behind me.

"An old woman. She's digging," I pointed, "there."

I watched as she pulled something from next to her legs. It was Hilda. The doll stared unseeing at the ceiling as the woman placed the doll in the hole.

"Our Father, who art in Heaven, hallowed be thy name," the woman began to mumble the Lord's Prayer as she shoveled dirt on top of the doll with her hands. With each handful of dirt, she emphasized her words. "…and forgive us our *trespasses*…" Another handful. "…but deliver us from *evil*…"

The last thing to be covered was the doll's eye. It peered out from the dirt and seemed to look right at me. I took a sharp breath in as the vision faded.

"You okay, Anderson?" Andy asked.

I stood there a moment before answering. "Yeah, yeah, I'm fine." I relayed what I saw. "Who do you think that was? And, why was she burying the doll?"

"Tristan said that this house was owned by an older couple before Kristen and Dalton moved in. Maybe it was her."

That felt right. I turned to look back at the corner. "Do you think the doll went to her like it goes to Hannah?"

Andy fake shivered. "I would've burned that doll a long time ago," he said, turning to walk back upstairs. "I'm going to check on the equipment and then I'm going to hit the pizza."

A set of images flashed through my mind. Kristen taking the doll to the Goodwill. Her taking it to the woods and leaving it on a tree stump. The image of her driving to a bridge and slinging the doll over her head into the churning water below. Kristen placing the doll into a pile of burning brush.

Ice ran down my spine. "She tried," I mumbled. *That's what she was hiding. And, that's why she's so afraid of it.*

Evie looked at me. "How are you feeling?" she asked.

"A little tired, but not like before. Not as drained."

"Good," she said. "Wanna go upstairs?"

I nodded, wanting to escape the feeling of dread that spread like a fungus across the floor of the basement.

Upstairs, Tristan and Andy placed all of the cameras and the audio feeds were already recording.

"What next, fearless leader?" I asked Andy as I sat down in a chair and grabbed a piece of pizza from the box. I wasn't hungry, but chewed on the end of the slice.

I stared at the monitor. It was filled with seven small screens, showing different areas of the house. There was the basement, two shots of Hannah's room, the crawlspace behind her closet, Kristen and Dalton's room, the living room, and a final shot that included the pantry area and the top of the stairs. "Looks good," I mentioned.

Andy nodded, his cheek pushed out with a huge bite of pizza. "We have good coverage. We can try the spirit box as soon as the doll shows up."

The way he said it made gooseflesh rise up along my arms.

"What makes him so sure that it'll show up?" Evie asked.

"Oh, right! You left before you heard about that. Even when Hilda goes missing through the day, she always appears in Hannah's room by the time she wakes up. Kristen seemed pretty weirded out by that."

"And, you wouldn't be?" Evie asked. She looked around the kitchen.

"It's not going to jump out of a cabinet and scare you," I said.

"What's wrong, Patton? Scared of the little doll?" Andy asked, shoving another half piece of pizza into his mouth. Evie threw him a glare.

I mulled it over for a moment. "I think the doll is trying to tell us something."

"Yeah, get out of the house before it kills us all." Andy widened his eyes.

"Not funny," Evie said. She looked pale.

"Lay off, Andy," I said. I turned to Evie. "Listen, it's normal to be afraid, but I don't think the doll is here to hurt us. I really do think it's trying to tell us something. We just have to figure out what it is."

Evie nodded, but kept her arms wrapped around her chest. "There's a disturbance here," she said. "I can see something pressing against the fabric."

"Can you tell where it's coming from?"

She shook her head. "No, only that it's coming from this place. The house or the land around the house." She shook her head. "It's hard for me to pinpoint it."

"Don't try," I said quickly. "Hang onto your energy." She nodded.

"Holy crap!" Tristan pointed at the monitor. "Where did she come from?"

Andy and I leaned in to look at the screen. Sitting on the pallet in the crawlspace behind the closet was Hilda. She sat with the skirt of her tattered dress spread out over her legs and as we watched, her head turned to look directly at the camera. The way the light played on the doll's features, she looked like she was pure evil.

I shuddered. "She wasn't there when we looked a second ago."

"And she wasn't up there when I placed the camera," Tristan said, his hands rubbing absently up and down his arms.

"Okay," I said. Then, "okay," again. "We have to go up there."

"Yep."

"Uh huh."

We all continued to stare at the doll on the screen. As we watched, the head of the doll appeared to turn slightly again.

"Did you see that?" Tristan put his hand over his mouth and stood up, nearly knocking the chair over behind him.

I tried to keep my voice even and calm. "We're going to go up there and see if we can figure out what she's trying to tell us. Someone should stay here and watch the monitor in case something happens somewhere else in the house."

Evie threw her hand up in the air. "That's me. I totally call that!"

"Chicken," I snorted.

"Yep. Bawk, bawk." She put her hands in her armpits and waved her elbows up and down. "I told you, I don't do dolls."

"Evie wants to stay here," I said.

"Tristan can stay with her," Andy said.

I looked at Evie. She looked sick and pale. "That may be a good idea."

She pressed her lips together. "No, I can't. I feel like I need to go with you."

"Fine. Come with Andy and me, but if you feel bad or get scared, come back down and sit with Tristan."

"Sure, St. Louis," she said, her eyes tight and her jaw set.

I stood up and pulled out my phone from my pocket.

Andy gathered a camera and the spirit box. He handed a walkie to Tristan and placed a hand on his shoulder. "Call if you need anything."

We headed through the kitchen and the living room, pausing at the bottom of the steps.

"I'll go first," I offered. I felt like a hand was pressed into the small of my back, pushing insistently, wanting me to get up to that room. I put my foot on the first tread and the sound of singing wound its way down to me from above. It was a little girl's voice. The goose bumps that retreated a moment before in the kitchen pricked at my skin again. I took a deep breath and began climbing. At the landing, I turned and placed my hand on the doorknob to Hannah's room.

"Ouch!" I cried, pulling my hand back like it was bitten.

Andy was immediately by my side. "What happened?" he asked, grabbing my hand and turning it to look at my palm.

I pulled my hand back from his grasp. "The doorknob's cold."

Andy held his hand an inch above it. "Wow," he breathed, the vapor spreading from his lips into a cloud. Pulling the backpack from his shoulder, he unzipped the small front pocket and took out a pair of gloves. He pulled one on and reached out to open the door.

It swung open into the little girl's room.

I stepped inside and the cold enveloped me, spreading to my arms and legs, making it hard to breathe. "Hilda, are you here?"

Andy placed his backpack on Hannah's bed and pulled out his old cell phone. He connected an external speaker to it and brought up a relaxation app. White noise filled the room. He looked up at me and nodded toward the closet.

I swallowed and looked back to check on Evie. She stood at the threshold of the room, her face unreadable.

"Hilda, my name is Andy and this is my friend Marissa and our friend Evie. Would you like to talk to us?"

The white noise came through, undulating for a moment before a voice came through; a high-pitched whisper that cut through the silence of the room. "Hilf mir."

I shivered. "I'm going into the closet," I announced, hoping that Andy or Evie would tell me what a colossally bad idea it was. *No, no, Marissa, it's too dangerous. Let me go instead.*

When no one said anything to deter me, I put the hem of my shirt over my hand and opened the closet door. Hannah's clothes swung gently on the pole, as if someone had recently walked through and disturbed them. I closed my eyes and got down on my hands and knees. I turned on my phone's flashlight and pointed it out in front of me as I crawled to the back of the closet. I could hear Andy at the door of the closet, and knowing he was close, it gave me a bit of bravery that I was running very short of at the moment.

"Hilda, are you in here?" I asked, pushing the hand with the flashlight into the space before I stuck my head in.

No amount of bravery could have prepared me for what I saw in that crawlspace.

CHAPTER 16

I cried out and dropped my phone, the LED light splashing wildly across the walls before it landed and skidded across the floor, landing at the feet of the little girl standing in the crawlspace. She had brown curly hair that was matted to the side of her head and her long white dress was torn and dirty. She held onto the doll fiercely and stared at me through sunken eyes.

"Marissa!" Andy shouted from the closet. "What's happening?"

"I'm fine," I called back, "hold on." I scooted into the small space and sat cross-legged on the floor, leaning to the side under the slanting wall. "Amalie?" I said softly. "Are you Amalie?"

The little girl nodded. She was shivering, and her lips were blue.

"Amalie, my name is Marissa and my friends and I are here to help you. Would you like us to help you?"

The little girl nodded and continued to stare out at me with baleful eyes. The doll's accusing eyes didn't blink.

"Is there something you want to show me?" I asked, my mind reeling.

Amalie nodded and sat down across from me. She wore one slipper and it was caked with mud. Her other foot was bare and covered with cuts. My heart ached for her. I could feel the coldness rolling off her and I shivered.

"I can see things that you want to show me," I said quietly. "You don't have to be afraid."

A moment later, the pressure descended upon me and I blinked away tears. The little girl sat in the crawlspace, her dress brand new and her curls bobbing as she leaned over her doll, brushing her hair. The doll was dressed impeccably and her bright eyes and rosy red cheeks stood out in contrast to her unblemished porcelain face. The little girl sang a song in German. It was the same song I'd heard so many times in the house and the song

Kristen told us that Hannah was singing. A voice came through the wall, "Amalie! Bettzeit."

"Ja, Mutter," the little girl called. She placed the doll on the floor and gathered her dress around her as she crawled out of the space. She reached past me to grab her doll and I followed her out of the closet past Andy. Evie stood in the doorway watching. I saw the mother helping Amalie out of her blue dress and into a long white sleeping dress. It fell to her ankles and had a sweet lace collar on it. Amalie climbed into the wrought iron bed next to the window, humming as she stroked the doll's cheek. Her mother sat behind the little girl, pulling a brush through her hair. She sang a song quietly as she began to braid Amalie's hair: "*Schlafe, mein Kindlein, schlaf ein. Am Himmel strahlen die Sternelein. Mache schnell die Aeuglein zu, So findest du deine Ruh.*"

She finished braiding the little girl's hair and stood up. Leaning over, she pulled the quilt up over Amalie and bent over her to kiss her on the forehead. "Ich liebe dich."

"Ich liebe dich auch."

The mother placed a hand on the child's cheek in a tender motion and I smiled. Amalie's mother loved her so much. She blew out the lantern next to the bed and walked out of the room. Some time passed and I watched as the moon moved along the night sky outside her window. There was a crash somewhere downstairs.

I turned to look at Andy. "What was that?"

He shook his head. "Not happening here, Anderson. I didn't hear anything."

I looked at Evie. She shook her head as well.

A few moments later, I heard a roaring noise from below. My feet grew hot as I stood in the middle of Hannah's room. "There's a fire!" I shouted. "Tristan!"

Andy ran out of the room and I could hear his shoes pounding down the stairs.

The walkie crackled in my hand. "Everything's quiet down here."

The roaring filled my consciousness and I blinked. The acrid smell of smoke began to creep into the room. Amalie's figure stirred. I turned to see the doll drop from her hands and land on the floor with a crash. The crack along the doll's cheek spread like a spider web from the place of impact. Amalie stirred, the sound of the doll dropping rousing her.

A moment later, her mother appeared at her door. "Feuer!" she shouted, rushing into the room and gathering Amalie into her arms. Amalie screamed; reaching out for her doll as her mother carried her from the room. The smoke billowed into the room. I stood watching for a moment and Amalie appeared again at her doorway. She ran in and picked up her doll, cradling it against her tear-streaked face. The heat rose, spreading white-hot fingers of smoke into my lungs. I began to cough.

"We need to get you out of here," Andy said quietly, taking my elbow in his hand. "Come on."

I nodded and let him lead me out of the room and down the stairs. I looked up and fell against Andy's side. "It's all on fire," I said, looking around. The kitchen was mostly gone at this point, completely consumed by flames. The father and son were trying to throw snow on the burning room and the mother ran into the backyard, a bucket of snow in her hands. She passed it through the door to the father who tossed it on the fire. The steam rose up, pressing in on them and forcing the mother and father out the back door. The son was trapped on the other side of the kitchen. The flames licked up the wall behind him, catching on the ceiling and spreading. He moved around the room, trapped by the sudden flame up.

I pressed my face into Andy's chest as the boy's screams rose up around me. "I can't watch this," I cried.

Andy yanked open the door and helped me out into the backyard. I gulped down the cold air, wanting to stop watching the awful events of this night, but knowing that Amalie needed me to see something. The mother and father began throwing bucketful after bucketful of snow onto the burning house. The roaring of the fire and the sobs of the mother were the only sounds I could hear.

"She's showing me the night of the fire," I said, hanging onto Andy for strength as I watched. Tristan came out of the kitchen, his body out of place amid waist high flames. Evie followed him, holding onto the door as she wavered on the porch steps.

"Amalie and her brother died in the fire. She went back for her doll and she didn't get out." I felt my knees give out and Andy held me up with a strong arm.

I backed up as the flames lit up the entire house and caught on the dry grass surrounding the house. The banks of snow kept the fire from alighting on the trees in the back. They were closer to the house than present day, not yet cleared out to create a bigger yard. The banks of snow created a circle, containing the fire that rose into the night sky. The father stopped shoveling and took his wife's hands in his. Tears ran through the soot on his face, as he peered at her. Her mouth was drawn open in a scream and she let out the saddest sound from somewhere within the depths of her soul.

I would never forget that sound. Not ever.

Tears ran down my face as I watched the man lead his grieving wife to the front of the house. A noise behind me made me turn around. Amalie emerged from the window on the back of the house, her white dress turned black by smoke and ash. She landed on the ground, rolling away from the fire, her hair tangling around her. When she stood up, she held her doll against her, as she turned and turned in the yard. "Mutter! Vater!" she cried into the night, but the roaring of the fire drowned out her cries.

The heat pressed me further back and Amalie moved back, too. She limped, her ankle twisted at an odd angle from the fall into the yard. I watched as she limped away from the house, into the edge of the forest. Her tear-filled eyes gleamed in the light of the fire and she continued to back away from the sight. "Mutter, Vater," she cried over and over again.

"She can't see them. She thinks they're still in the house." I felt my insides crush. "She thinks she's all alone."

Amalie turned around and looked into the forest behind her. She seemed to make her mind up about something and began to walk.

"We have to follow her," I said. "I think she's trying to find help."

"The nearest neighbor on that side is over five miles away," Tristan said, looking at his phone. "It's all forest through here."

"Maybe that's the only neighbor there was back then," Evie said.

I set my jaw and followed the little girl as she moved through the thick underbrush. The moonlight cut through the limbs of the trees above, the silver light slicing down to the forest floor. Amalie walked for a long time, her teeth chattering and her lips turning a nasty shade of blue. I watched as she climbed over a huge log, only to fall into a marshy area on the other side. She came up covered in mud, her hair matted to the side of her head.

"She went through so much," I mumbled. "She was so scared and cold."

Amalie pressed on, winding her way through patches of brambles that snagged at her hair and dress, ripping it. Long lines of red rose up on her legs and blood poured from her wounds. At one point, she almost dropped the doll, but she managed to hold onto it. I could hear her begin to breathe heavily and the chattering of her teeth intensified. She stood in the middle of the trees and looked around. She shook her little head and began walking, winding back the way she came in a large circle.

"She's confused," I whispered. "I think she's freezing."

The icy air pressed in on me and I was thankful when I felt a coat draped over my shoulders. I glanced at Tristan and nodded, and put my eyes back on Amalie. She was again trying to make her way over an enormous log. Her little hands pulled at the rough bark, breaking open and bleeding. She lost her grip and fell on the other side, her leg twisting beneath her. I watched as Amalie lay there in the snow next to the doll, her breathing becoming shallower and shallower. She stared up at the sky between the trees and her lips parted. She began to sing, the song halting and barely a whisper.

"Mache schnell...die Aeuglein...zu...So findest...du deine...Ruh..."

I sat down on the ground next to her small figure. I reached out my hand and placed it on hers. The frigidness spread into my palms and I tried to send her some warmth, some comfort. *You're not alone now, Amalie. We're here. You're not alone.*

Tears streamed down my face as I watched the light leave her little eyes. She died staring up at the stars.

I shook my head and looked up at Andy and Tristan. They stood next to one another, Andy's arm wrapped around Tristan's shoulders. They both had tears in their eyes. Evie stood back a bit, her body almost transparent.

"She died here," I said, standing up. "She was all alone."

"Her parents thought she died in the fire," Tristan said. He walked over to me. "How are you?"

I nodded. "I'm tired." I hesitated. "And sad." I turned around and looked at the spot where Amalie died. Some of the huge log was still there, the lower part petrified by lying in water for all these years. The snow had been disturbed and I knelt down, beginning to dig at the snow and dirt.

"I'll get a shovel from the house," Andy said grimly. He trudged back the way we came.

I sat back on my feet. "How far are we from the house?" I asked.

Tristan looked at his phone. "We're only a quarter mile from the house. She almost made it back home."

I didn't know if this made it better or worse. I felt completely drained and numb.

Evie came over and knelt next to me. "She's here, St. Louis. Have her buried with her family. She won't be lonely anymore."

"You have to go, don't you?" I asked.

Evie nodded. "I used a lot of energy tonight." She bit her bottom lip. "Energy I didn't have to spend." She stood up. "I'll see you tomorrow morning?"

I stood up. "Of course, Evie. I'll be there."

"Later, St. Louis," she said.

I watched as my best friend turned and began walking, fading into the night.

Andy returned a few minutes later, carrying a shovel over his shoulder. It took him a few scoops into the earth to find what we were looking for.

I took a sharp breath in as the moonlight glinted off a long white bone.

CHAPTER 17

I called Kristen while Andy and Tristan put away all the equipment. I told her that we found the remains of a little girl on the property and that we needed to alert the authorities.

"I'm coming home," she said into the phone.

We took all of the equipment out to the truck and sat around the kitchen table, the silence spreading out between us. The house felt lighter, airier somehow.

Kristen arrived shortly after nine, a sleeping Hannah in tow. She took her upstairs and laid her on her bed. She came back downstairs and handed the doll to me. "This belonged to the little girl, didn't it?"

I nodded.

Kristen looked down at the doll and smoothed its dress down gently. "You should make sure it gets back to her." She handed it to me.

"What about Hannah?" I asked.

"She has other dolls." Her jaw was set.

I sat down at the table and told Kristen what we found out about the house. Her eyes gleamed with tears when I related the story of who we thought had been haunting the house and how Amalie died.

She took a deep breath and wiped at her eyes. "Show me?"

Andy and I took Kristen out the back door to where Amalie's body lay. Tristan waited at the house in case Hannah woke up.

"We need to call the police," Kristen said. "I'm going to call Dalton and have him come home."

"What are you going to tell him?" I asked.

She took a deep breath. "That I went out for a walk and I found her here."

"We should go," I said. I stood for a moment, uncomfortable silence wedging between us.

Kristen smiled sadly. "You helped," she said.

I looked up at her and nodded, the lump in my throat keeping me from talking. *It doesn't feel like enough.*

"Thank you," Kristen said. She showed us to the door and waited until we were in the truck before she raised the phone to her ear and closed the door behind her.

"Do you think they'll bury her next to her parents?" I asked.

"I'll make sure of it," Tristan said. He was on his phone, typing an email.

"What are you doing?" I asked, masking an enormous yawn behind my hand.

"Contacting her family. If they claim the remains, it will move the process along. They can probably get her buried by tomorrow if her family puts enough pressure on them."

"Oh," I said. It was all my exhausted mind could muster at that point. I looked down at the doll in my lap. She was looking up at me with her glass eyes. They were the last thing I saw before I fell asleep in Andy's truck.

***

The next morning, Dad came into my room and sat on the edge of my bed, his coffee cup sending up warm steam around his stubbly face as he took a sip. He sucked a breath in through his teeth and nodded at the doll that sat on my desk.

"What's that?" he asked.

I sat up, rubbing my eyes. "It belongs to a little girl who died a long time ago," I said, the sleep making my voice gruff and my words slur.

"Your group didn't have anything to do with the human remains found on a farm last night, did it?"

"How did you hear about that?"

"I have a friend on the police department. Wanna talk about it?" he asked.

I thought about telling him about Amalie, but I felt my throat close with emotion. I shook my head. "Not right now, but I will, I promise."

"I know," he said. He looked over at me. "You coming to the hospital this morning with me?"

I smiled. "Yeah, I'll come over for a bit." I wanted to see Evie and let her know what happened after she left.

Dad furrowed his brow at me and then smiled. "Sounds good. I'll be there for a little bit, but then I have to go pick up Genevieve's dad."

I got ready in record time and I was heading to the truck with my dad when my phone beeped. I pulled it out of my coat pocket and looked down.

Grant: *New Year's. My house? 8 p.m.? Bring friends.*

"Dad, can Evie and I go to Grant's New Year's Eve party?"

He gave me a puzzled look from behind the steering wheel. "Yeah, um, yeah. That would be fine."

I didn't realize until we started on the highway that I said Evie was going as well. I texted Grant to let him know I would be there.

When we got to the hospital, we headed upstairs to Evie's room. I looked around the room. Evie wasn't there. A doctor stood next to her bed, his face grim as we entered the room.

"What's wrong?" Dad asked.

"Her O-two levels have almost bottomed out," the doctor said. "Maybe your daughter should step out for a moment?"

"No, she can stay. What do we do now?"

The doctor glanced at me. "We need to start thinking about what would be best for Genevieve," he said, his voice dropping in volume with each word.

Dad's eyes flashed. "What's best for Genevieve is that she comes out of this coma and comes home with us. Now, I understand that you have to prepare for the worst, but we are not ready to write her off."

The doctor placed the clipboard back on the bed and nodded, shoving his hands deep into the pockets of his white lab coat. "We will continue to monitor her and we'll keep doing everything we can, but with her readings, her body is in great distress."

When the doctor left, my dad sat down on the chair heavily.

I walked around and placed a hand on his shoulder. "It's going to be okay. I promise."

He reached his hand up and placed it over mine. "I know, Peanut."

We waited quietly together until Dad had to leave to go pick up Evie's father. I didn't leave her side. The feeling of watching her wasting away reminded me so much of when my mother was in a hospital bed like this one, unable to help as her body betrayed her from the inside out.

"Evie," I whispered, leaning in over her body, "I know you're not in there right now, but I really need you to wake up soon." Tears threatened and I closed my eyes against them.

The morning wore on and turned to afternoon. Dad returned with Evie's father. He was an older version of the man I saw in my visions and he looked tired and weary. He came into the room and walked over to his daughter, his breath catching in his throat as he leaned down over her and brushed her hair from the bandage on her forehead. Pulling a chair up to the bed, he held onto her hand as he sat there, talking quietly to her, his eyes full of concern and quiet regret.

Dad guided me out of the room by my shoulder. "We should give them some time," he said, his voice full of emotion. "This could be the last time he gets to see her."

I felt a ball of white hot anger growing in my stomach. "You've already given up on her," I said, "just like you did when Mom died."

Dad winced and I immediately regretted the words. He rubbed a hand across his chin, the stubbly sound echoing in the hallway. His eyes fixated on the painting next to me in the hallway. It was a copy of *Water Lilies* but had too much yellow in it, making it look like someone had thrown up on the canvas and then affixed it to the wall. I hated that painting.

When his eyes came back to rest on me, they weren't full of anger or hurt like I expected, but soft and full of love. "Marissa, I understand that you are hurting. I believe that Genevieve will come out of this, but I don't want you to be unprepared if she doesn't. When your mom got sick, I knew she was going to fight it. And, I told you that she was going to be all right. I regret that now. I should have prepared you better for the end." He took a deep breath. "Maybe it would have helped."

"You couldn't help me because you were always with her."

He nodded slowly. "I see what this is about. Marissa, I was with your mother at the hospital because she needed me, like Genevieve needs me now." He held up a hand when I opened my mouth. "I understand that you can see her and she's not in her body, but she knows that

I'm here. She sees me and she knows that there is one person that will never give up on her."

I swallowed the lump in my throat hard. I blinked.

"She's never had that before. Everyone has always given up on her. She doesn't deserve that and I want her to know that I'm here. That's important to me."

I nodded. "It's important to me, too. I understand why you're here all the time. I'm sorry I said that. I didn't mean it, and I don't think anything would have made losing Mom any easier. I think the hope that she would get better kept me from going crazy while she was sick." I leaned back against the wall and folded my arms across my chest. "I don't want to give up on Evie. She's going to get better."

"She will. We have to know that she's going to come back. Now, I'm going to go down and get some coffee. You want anything?"

I shook my head. "I'm fine, thanks."

He waited a moment before starting to walk, his eyes never leaving my face. I avoided his gaze. Anger still swelled around me, but worse than that, doubt began crowding into my mind, blocking everything out. *What if Sam couldn't figure out how to get her back to her body? What would happen if her body died? She'd be a ghost,* I answered myself. *My best friend would be gone and I would only have an imprint of what she was.* I shook my head, the tears beginning to spill out. I didn't want her to die. A ghost wasn't what I wanted. I wanted my friend. I wanted the laughs, the tears, and the fights. I wanted my best friend.

As I stood sentry next to the door. I could hear Evie's dad talking to her. His voice carried out into the quiet hallway. *I shouldn't listen. It's rude.* I leaned in, his voice becoming clearer.

"…Genevieve, I loved your mother and you so very much. I wanted you to come stay with me in Austin. I sent your mother money every month and letter after letter. I didn't want you to grow up thinking I didn't love or miss you. I sent her plane tickets every single summer and waited at the airport for the plane to come in, but you were never on it. I don't know what she told you, Genevieve, but I loved you then and I will always love you."

"Then, why didn't you come back?" I opened the door and stood in the space, my anger spilling out into the room in waves. "Do you know what she went through in her mother's house? How could you have left her with that…that *monster?*"

Evie's father looked up at me as if I struck him. He stared out at me through the mire of sadness and regret that surrounded his very being. His mouth moved but no sound came out. Then, he looked down and placed his hand on Evie's arm. When he looked up at me again, his eyes were full of tears. "I *had* to leave. If I stayed, I would have started drinking again and I would have hurt one of them."

"I get why you thought you had to leave, but why didn't you come back?"

He peered at me, sizing me up. "Your father asked me the same question."

I came around the bed and sat down in the chair on the other side of Evie's bed. I sat down and stared across my sleeping friend at him. "What did you tell *him*?"

Jeff continued to hold Evie's arm, his thumb rubbing her arm through the sheet in a comforting motion. Finally, he shook his head. "Not the truth."

"Fine. What is the truth then?"

"The truth is I think something evil was following me while I was here in Culvers Grove." When I didn't react, he went on. "It was like I was being turned evil. That sounds stupid. It was like something evil was taking over. When I drove out of town that morning, my truck shuddered as I crossed the boundary outside of town. Something hit the back of my truck and it scared me to death. I drove and kept on driving. I was driving away from the evil thing in this town." He looked up at me. "Does that sound crazy?"

"No, it doesn't." I wondered for a moment if I should tell him about what I saw in Evie's memory, but then I decided he didn't deserve the truth yet. "When did the feeling start?" I asked instead.

He sat back in the chair and rubbed the back of his neck. "I guess it started right after Genevieve's mother and I moved into the house together. I started working at the quarry and…" he trailed off, his eyes coming up to meet mine. They were wide and unwavering. "I remember when it started. We set up to blow out a cliff side for a large order of gravel for the city. I did the face survey and the drilling contractor drilled the shot holes. Everything went as planned, but I somehow missed a cave tributary running right alongside the quarry that none of us knew about. It was missed on all of the audits. Anyway, as the dust from the blast was settling, I remember something dark rushing out at me through the opening. I remember putting my hands up to shield my face. I thought it was a secondary explosion. The darkness hit me and I felt cold and hot, and angry."

He looked up at me and I nodded for him to go on.

Jeff cleared his throat. "Anyway, I brushed it off because I thought I was upset that I missed such a large hollow. I'd put everyone on the blast scene in danger. We checked the shot pile for undetonated devices and then checked the hollow area. It spread back as far as we could see and it felt," he looked up at me again, "um, well, it felt evil. Anyway, I went home that night and Genevieve's mother and I fought over something stupid, probably money and I took off and went to the bar." He held up his hand, "I didn't drink. We'd been clean and sober since we found out Tammy was pregnant. I ordered a scotch and it sat in front of me until all the ice melted and then I went home."

"What happened after that?" I asked. *How had this turned into the last memory Evie showed me?*

"Things got worse. I was sick all the time. I couldn't eat. I couldn't sleep. Tammy and I were fighting like cats and dogs, and then one day, I was at the quarry and I started hearing voices."

"Voices?"

He nodded, his eyes guarded. "They told me to kill Tammy and Genevieve."

My hand flew up to my mouth.

Jeff glanced around furtively. "Please don't tell anyone that. I don't why I told you." He put his hands up to his temples and rested his head in his hands.

"What are you going to do now?" I asked.

He looked up at me again, his eyes deeper set than they had been a moment before. "I don't know. I thought I could come back here. I mean, I *had* to come back here for Genevieve." He leaned up again and took her hand in his. "I should have come before this. I didn't know what was going on, and I should have been here."

If he was waiting for me to argue with him on this point, he was going to be waiting a long time. Now I understood why he left and why he never came back. Whatever was released from that cave had attached itself to him and he left to keep his family safe. I squinted at him as he looked down at his daughter. I couldn't see anything, but then, I leaned back in my chair and peered under the chair. My skin began to crawl.

There, around his feet, a black mist swirled, caressing his legs like it found a long-lost friend. I stood up and backed away from him as my dad came through the door.

Jeff stood up as well and pulled his jacket from the chair behind him. "If you don't mind, John, can you take me to my hotel? I'm not feeling very well."

Dad nodded. "I'll be back soon," he said to me. They left the room and I stood at the end of Evie's bed as the door shut behind me.

"Thanks, St. Louis."

The voice made me jump. I whirled around and saw Evie standing near the closed door. Her hair hung limply over her shoulders and there was no sparkle in her eyes.

"You don't look very good, Evie."

She managed a small laugh. "Gee, thanks. You look like crap, too."

"You know what I mean. I don't think you have very much time left."

She looked at her body wistfully. "I know. I can feel it. The tie isn't as strong anymore." She glanced at me. "I can feel a tie between myself and my body. It's fading."

Her words made ice race through my arms. "Evie, you need to get back into your body. What did Sam find out?"

She smiled, her eyes gentle. "He found out what he needed to know and he's getting things ready. He says he thinks I'll be back in my body by tomorrow morning."

"Seriously! You could be back by tomorrow!" My smile was genuine and I felt like a weight was lifted from my chest. "Evie, that's amazing. Can we do anything to help?"

"Just be here when I wake up?"

"Of course, I'll be here first thing in the morning. Can Andy and Tristan come, too?" Giddiness spread through me, then doubt. "What is Sam going to do?"

"Yes, they can come, and I don't know. He said he has to meet with the person one more time today to get the details, but he sounded really excited. They're going to help me, St. Louis." She stared down at her body. "And, it looks like it can't come too soon." She shook her head and looked up at me. "Anyway, I came here to tell you that, but I need to go soon."

"How long have you been here?"

"Long enough to hear what you said to my dad."

"Listen, I'm sorry. I shouldn't have done that. I should have waited for you and made sure you wanted me to ask those questions."

She smiled sadly. "It's fine. I'm glad you asked. I don't know that I could have."

"So," I started, "what are you going to do now?"

"Well," she crossed the room and sat down on the windowsill, the afternoon sun passing through her almost transparent frame, "now that I know why he left, I don't think he should stay here. I think that as soon as I wake up, he should go back to Austin. It's not safe for him to be here."

I bit my bottom lip. "Are you going to go with him?"

She looked at me for a long time. "I thought about it. I really did, but that's not where my home is."

"You can't go to your mom's again, Evie. Not after how she's been to you, you can't possibly think…"

"Are you kidding me? I would never go back to her trailer. I meant my *home.*"

The word resonated with me. *Home.* It hadn't been that long ago that I didn't think I would ever call the farm home, but over the past few months, it had become my home. And Evie's as well. I smiled. "I'm glad."

My phone buzzed in my pocket. It was Tristan. "He says that they are burying Amalie's bones this evening. Do you want to go with us?"

She shook her head. "I should get back to Sam. I'll see you later?"

I smiled. "Yeah, tomorrow morning. I'll be here."

"Me, too," she said and then walked through the hospital door.

CHAPTER 18

I left Dad at the hospital and met Andy and Tristan downstairs. Before heading to the cemetery, we made a quick stop by my house to pick up the doll. "It needs to be with Amalie now," I said, climbing back into the seat with the doll resting in the crook of my arm.

I told Andy and Tristan about what happened at the hospital earlier and how Evie had come to talk to me. "She said she would be back in her body by tomorrow morning."

Tristan glanced at Andy and then took my hand in his. They were warm and comforting. I could feel my hand vibrating with nervous energy in his. "Marissa, how are they going to get her back in her body?"

I blinked. "Um, she didn't say how. She told me that he talked to someone and they knew how to do it." I immediately felt stupid for not asking about the details. "I guess I was so excited that I didn't ask."

Tristan patted my hand. "We understand, but Andy and I have been talking, and if this doesn't work and Evie doesn't make it, we need to know that you're going to be okay."

"Yeah," Andy said. "We don't want to have to visit you at the funny farm."

"Ignore him."

"No," I withdrew my hand from the cocoon of warmth and placed it in my lap. "He's right. This whole thing seems so surreal, and I know that you guys don't trust Sam, and I didn't at first either, but I don't think we have any choice now. If he says he knows how to help, he will."

"How do you know that?" Andy asked, flipping on the turn signal as he turned onto the gravel road to the cemetery. The afternoon sun's rays glowed orange through the scraggly trees alongside the road.

"I know because Evie believes in him. She trusts him and that's all I need to know."

"We're worried about you, Anderson," Andy said.

"I'll be fine." *I always am.* Their words dug into the bubble of doubt inside me, pulling at it, causing the questions to run out in torrents through my mind. I swallowed, biting them back. "She's going to be fine, too. If you guys don't believe Sam can do it, why did you agree to come tomorrow morning then?"

"We want to be there for you, your dad, and Evie. We believe she's going to come out of this, too, but we're trying to be realistic. I mean, you have to admit that it sounds pretty far-fetched. Who did Sam go talk to and what did the person tell him about how to get Evie back into her body?"

I sat in silence for a long time, letting Tristan's question roll around in my head. I clung to the doll. It was cold against my skin.

"Tell them that Sam is going to make the curtain thin for me."

I almost jumped out of my skin and whipped around to look behind me. Evie sat in the bed of the truck, her eyes resting on the back of Andy's head as the truck flew down the road.

"What are you doing here?"

"Thought you could use some help. They're a little more cynical about things than you and I are."

"Marissa? What's going on?" Tristan stared at me.

"Evie's here. She says that Sam figured out how to make the curtain between the worlds thin so she can get through - back to her body."

"How?"

I turned. "I thought you went to meet Sam."

"I have a bit of time. He's still meeting with the person."

"Who is the person?"

Evie bit her bottom lip.

"You can tell me."

"It's a really, really old ghost from before the town was built. It's the oldest ghost in Culvers Grove."

"And Sam is talking to him? I didn't think he could leave City Hall."

"He's close enough for Sam to talk to. That's all he told me."

"So, how is he going to make the curtain thin?"

"That's what we want to know," Andy mumbled.

Tristan shushed him and turned to look at the truck bed.

"He says that we are supposed to allow me to die."

"What?" I shouted.

Tristan and Andy jumped.

"It's how the soul leaves the body. When a person's body dies, the veil thins around them, allowing their soul to move to another place. If my body dies, then I can move through in the opposite way."

"No, that's too dangerous! There has to be another way!"

"What'd she say?"

I relayed the information to Tristan and he began shaking his head. "No way. That's crazy, Evie."

"Not really." Andy slowed the truck and pulled it to the side of the road near a bank of snow. He turned around in his seat and looked at the bed of the truck.

"Are you serious right now?" Tristan's voice held exasperation.

"I am. It makes sense. If someone passes away, the veil thins to let the soul out. It can also allow something in."

"But her body will be *dead*," I said. "She won't have anything to go back to."

"Once her soul goes back in her body, it will be alive again. The timing would have to be precise, though." Andy ran a hand over his chin. "Too long and she won't have a viable body to get back into." His eyes flitted to the bed of the truck again. "That's why you wanted us there, isn't it? To pull the plug?"

"Not exactly," Evie said.

"Oh, Evie," I breathed. "You know you're dying, don't you?" My eyes flooded with tears.

She nodded. "It's going to be soon, St. Louis."

"What happens if you get back in your body and something's wrong with it?" I asked, my voice trembling.

"We'll cross that bridge when we come to it. For now, I only have to worry about getting back in my body. Sam is going to help me get ready. I'm going to be with him."

"You don't want to leave him."

"I wish there was a way he could come with me."

I closed my eyes. "Evie, I'm so sorry." When I opened them again, she was gone. I sighed. "She loves him," I said to the boys, "and she has to say goodbye to him now."

Andy started the truck and started moving again. The cab was quiet the rest of the way out to the cemetery. When we passed by the first time, there was an older model Buick parked in the space near the road and two people stood silhouetted against the setting sun as they stood near a grave. A yellow backhoe was parked near the grave along with a trailer full of dirt. Andy continued to drive and turned around when the road allowed. The next time we passed by, the car was gone and the backhoe was moving, lifting piles of dirt from the trailer and dumping it onto the grave. Andy pulled in and we watched for a few minutes.

"Are you scared?" Tristan asked. "It's okay if you are."

It reminded me of one of the first times the Ghost Hunters Society had gone out on an investigation. He supported me when I was so scared, hurt, and unsure. I smiled in his direction. "No, Evie's strong and Sam would never do anything to hurt her. I think he loves her, too. Tomorrow morning, this will all go away and Evie will be back with us."

We watched the backhoe finish up and then it drove to the back of the cemetery and parked. The trailer pulled in next to it and then a man got out and stepped into a truck. He fired it up and bumped along the frozen ground to the remains of the road. He jostled past us, stopping to roll his window down. He leaned out over his arm and tipped the bill of his hat.

Andy rolled his window down, too.

"You kids lost?"

Andy shook his head. "No, sir, came by to visit my grandma. Wanted to wait until you were done."

The man squinted out the windshield at the gathering dusk. "Better hurry, don't want to be here when it's dark."

"Thank you," Andy said as the man rolled away. He rolled up his window and opened the door. "Ready?"

I nodded and got out the passenger door. Tristan slid out the driver's side and we shut the doors, the slamming the only sound in the quiet evening. We walked up the familiar path to the cemetery and opened the gate. The last time we were there, I was scared to death and heard someone telling me to get out. This time, though, the area felt quiet, sated. I made my way around headstones to the back part of the cemetery, Andy and Tristan following behind, arms linked, and their feet falling on the uneven ground.

When I reached the Schmidt family's graves, I peered down at the freshly disturbed gravesite. The simple cross stood quietly jutting up into the sky. I reached down and placed the doll on the ground, leaning her against the cross and smoothing her skirt down around her legs. Stepping back, I closed my eyes and tried to feel around for a vision of Amalie. A warm feeling started in my core and spread.

Tristan stepped up beside me. "Should we say something?"

I smiled. "Yeah, we should." I knelt down in front of the grave and placed my hand on the cold earth. "Amalie Schmidt, you are returned to your family. I hope that you find peace with them after all of these years. You're not alone anymore."

"That was nice," Tristan said as we walked back to the truck.

The wind picked up and raced around us, kicking up sparkles of snow in its wake. It whipped through the frozen limbs of the trees, sending up a wailing sound as we got back to the truck. I opened the door and began to step into the cab when I froze, my eyes wide.

"What's wrong?" Andy asked. "You look like you saw a ghost."

"No," I shook my head, "but I think I just heard one."

CHAPTER 19

"I don't understand," I huffed up the hill toward the forest, the wailing sound spreading out around me through the night.

"Can you not understand a little slower?" Andy huffed from behind me. The beam of his flashlight waved in crazy arcs as he struggled up the embankment with his backpack.

"We helped Mary. This can't be her, can it?" I spun around and looked at Andy and Tristan.

"Maybe we only thought we helped her." Tristan offered.

I shook my head. "No, I *saw* her leave with Matthias. They walked off into the forest together, holding hands. She finally helped him and got to be with him."

"There was a lot going on that night, you know," Andy said. He stopped and stood with his hand on his hip, his head tilted back as he tried to catch his breath. "You should start training for the Olympics. Speed walking's a sport, isn't it?"

"Andy's right," Tristan said. "Evie was hurt and we were trying to get her to the hospital."

"And, you thought you saw that black thing on the other side of the bridge."

I looked at him. "Say that again." Something was beginning to coalesce in my head.

"What? You thought you saw that black thing?"

I nodded. "Yeah, what if that black thing was the same thing that I saw attached to Evie's dad? What if it's something evil that can inhabit a person? Make them do things they normally wouldn't?"

"Like make someone want to kill their family?"

"Exactly. Jeff said that a dark cloud came out of the cave. What if it was the same thing we saw in Mary that night before Evie pushed it out of her?"

Andy tilted his head. "A dark cloud that can take over a human and a ghost?"

"Why not? What if it affects the soul instead of the body?"

"You said it affected Evie's mom? Do you think that's why she's so awful?" Tristan asked.

I thought back to the memory. I remembered the black mist touching her hand as she pushed Evie's dad out the front door. I remembered how it snaked along her arm and then dissipated. "I don't think so. I think it may have touched her, but I don't think it *made* her tell Evie's dad to leave. I don't think it caused her to take a drink that day or every day after that. I kind of wish it was, though. It would make it easier if we could blame her mother's behavior on some bad force."

"Right?"

"Yeah, unfortunately, I think Evie's mom made those decisions on her own. I *don't* think Evie's dad was going to be able to make his own decisions much longer, though. Whatever was influencing him was really taking hold. By the time he left Evie and her mom, he was in pretty bad shape."

"But, he still made the decision to leave. So, whatever was influencing him didn't have that strong a hold on him," Andy said.

"So, if something evil was attached to him, why?"

"I don't know," I said. "Maybe it was looking for a body."

"Then why take over a ghost? What was it looking for in Mary?"

"I don't know," I said again. My head was beginning to hurt from the onslaught of the sound of weeping. I had to make it stop soon or my eardrums felt like they were going to burst. "Come on."

They followed me through the woods to the creek. We wound our way down to the banks, the weeping carrying through the entire scope of my existence. I felt sick.

"Oh, my gosh," Tristan said. He pointed to the bridge. It was missing boards and looked like it would fall into the water with a solid push. "What happened?"

"Maybe when it flooded, something hit it and destroyed it?" Andy offered.

I shook my head. "It looks like something mangled it."

"Or some*one*," Andy said.

The thought sent shivers along my spine. "Do you think we can still get across?" I made my way down to the bridge and placed my hand on a post. The weeping sound stopped and the silence let me breathe again.

Andy walked over and set his backpack down on the bank. He shined the flashlight on the bridge and considered it for a moment. "I think it will hold. At least Marissa anyway."

I rolled my eyes. "Seriously?"

"Hey, not my fault you're the smallest."

Tristan tossed a severe look at Andy. "She's not going alone."

"I know," Andy said. "Trying to lighten the mood."

I took a breath and swiped the flashlight from his hand. "Fine, I'll go across first. Promise you'll follow?"

Andy and Tristan both nodded.

I placed a foot on the uneven boards and pressed down with some of my weight. The board creaked, but held. Picking my way across gingerly, I finally made it to the other side and started breathing again.

"Like a ninja," Andy said.

Tristan was next, his steps light on the precarious footing. When he made it to my side, Andy started. The bridge creaked and twisted dangerously and he jumped back.

"Put your backpack down. That thing must weigh fifty pounds."

Andy nodded, his eyes wide. "Yeah, yeah, the backpack." He shrugged it off his shoulders and placed it on the ground near a tree. This time, although the bridge groaned in protest, he was able to pick his way across. "That sucked," he said.

I looked back at the bridge, illuminated in the silvery moonlight. The image of Evie being pushed over the side into the churning water came back to me and I took a deep breath. The sound of her face crashing into the side of the bridge and the blood as it ran from the gash in her forehead brought tears to my eyes. "Let's go," I said, turning away from the bridge and starting to climb the embankment on the other side.

When we reached the clearing, the house rose up into the quiet night as it had the last time we were here. This time, though, the house looked more decrepit somehow, less cared for, lonelier. I shuddered in the cold night air, my breath rising around me in a mist.

"Does it look *different?*" Tristan hissed next to me.

I nodded. "Yeah, something's different." I closed my eyes and reached out, feeling for a spirit's energy. Near the back corner of the house, I located it. "Someone's here."

"Who is it?" Tristan breathed.

"I don't know. I can't tell." I started toward the house and Andy grabbed my arm.

"Let me go first. If something happens, you and Tristan run to the truck." He tossed the keys to Tristan.

"We're not leaving you here," Tristan said.

"If something happens, you're not going to stay." Andy strode toward the house, his feet making tracks in the dusting of snow in the clearing.

Tristan grabbed my hand and we followed; our breaths shallow as we listened for any sound, our eyes wide as we looked for any sign of movement.

"Where is it?" Andy said when he got to the front porch.

I closed my eyes and focused. "The kitchen."

Andy nodded and disappeared through the front door. Tristan and I climbed the front porch steps and stood in the doorway.

Andy picked his way along the sides of the caving in floor of the parlor. His feet knocked dust up from the floor in front of the fireplace and he sneezed, the sound echoing in the empty house. He made it to the doorway of the kitchen and stopped, shining his flashlight into every corner of the room. "Empty," he said.

I'm here.

I shook and Tristan looked at me questioningly.

I'm HERE!

"Mary?" I asked, creeping into the living room to stand next to Andy. I peered around his shoulder and saw her.

She sat in a chair by the kitchen table, her features gaunt and filled with sadness. Her hair was drawn into a bun, but it was shot through with gray and tendrils spilled out around her face. Her white dress was covered in dirt and ripped along the bottom, her bare feet muddy beyond the hem.

I stepped around Andy and stood in front of her, my hands on the slanting table. "What happened?" Tears burned the backs of my eyes. "We helped you."

Her eyes met mine, blazing with anger and sadness. *At least I could see him before. Now, he is gone yet I remain here. Alone.*

The word *alone* carried with it the sound of heartbreak. I took a hitching breath. "I don't understand. When we helped you pull him up from the bridge, I saw you walk away with him. I thought you were finally together."

We were. For but a moment. It was the most beautiful moment.

Her eyes took on a wistful quality and I watched her change into the beautiful young woman she once was, her hair shining and black, her dress ivory and pristine. That faded and the wretched shell of a woman sat before me again.

Then, he kissed me and faded away. I do not know where he has gone. I looked for him. At the house. The bridge. The forest. Her voice cracked and a tear spilled down her cheek, winding its way down and splashing on her dress. *I cannot find him.* She opened her mouth and the wailing sound filled the small room. I clapped my hands over my ears.

"What's going on, Anderson?"

"She can't find Matthias. He moved on and she didn't." I looked at Mary as the weeping sound wound down into a choked sob. "Mary, why didn't you move on with Matthias?"

I do not know. Will you help me find him?

My heart broke with her request. "I don't think he's here anymore." I turned around and looked at Andy. "Do you think the black thing kept her here?"

Andy shrugged. "I don't know."

"Mary, do you remember the night we were here and you tried to push me off the bridge?"

She gazed at me for a long time. Then, she shook her head. *I remember trying to pull Matthias from the noose. The rope was burning my hands. Then you were there, and then he was there. I did not push you from the bridge.*

"She doesn't remember anything about the black thing."

Help me, she moaned. *Please, help me. It hurts every single moment.*

I ground my nails into my palms. "I know how that feels. I really do, but I don't know how to help. Can you move on? Is there, I don't know, a white light anywhere? Something pulling you toward the other side?"

She stared at me. Her eyes grew hard and she stood up. *You should go now.*

"I want to help you."

Mary glanced behind her. When she turned, her eyes were wild. *You should go...NOW!*

"What are you afraid of? We want to help!" I felt so helpless and didn't want to leave until I knew why she was still here.

Now! She brought her hands up and then down in a raking motion. The house trembled around us and a deluge of dust and wood bits fell to the floor, skittering across the wood near our feet.

Andy grabbed my arm. "We need to go," he said. He pulled me across the floor and out the front door. The last thing I saw was Mary standing at the doorway of the kitchen. She cast an angry look my way, and as we passed onto the front porch, the door slammed shut behind us.

I turned and looked at Andy. "We have to help her!"

As I said this, the house shuddered, throwing the porch askew on its foundation. It tilted, throwing us off balance and we tumbled onto the front lawn as the house creaked and groaned, falling in on itself as the roof caved in. The remaining glass in the top window on the side shattered, sending shards of glass into the snow below.

"I don't think we can help her right now," Andy said, standing up and then pulling me to my feet.

"We need to leave," Tristan said. He nodded toward the house as it shuddered once more.

Mary stood in the window of the parlor, her eyes dark and filled with hate. She opened her mouth and let out a screeching sound as the house collapsed in on itself, sending dust spreading out in a cloud in the clearing.

Tristan, Andy, and I started running toward the bridge, the sound of cracking wood and the implosion chasing us into the trees. I stopped at the crest of the hill and turned around. The house was a pile of rubble, dust still rising into the moonlit night. The sound of weeping followed me all the way to the bridge where we crossed more quickly this time. Andy grabbed his backpack from its spot by the tree and we ran out of the forest on the other side. We climbed into the truck, and Andy twisted the key that Tristan handed him in the ignition. The engine caught and his headlights flooded the road with light.

Tristan turned the heat up full blast and reached over to make sure my vent was pointed on me. He slid the belt over me and clicked it, pulling to check that it was tight as Andy backed the truck out and onto the road.

As he turned, the headlights swung over the cemetery and I saw the eyes of the doll glint in the light.

CHAPTER 20

"We didn't help her," I said for what must have been the twentieth time since getting in the truck and heading back to my house. "What went wrong?"

"It's easier when you pass out after seeing a ghost," Andy mumbled, navigating his truck onto the highway that led to my house.

"She's upset," Tristan said. "And, the truth is, I am, too. We were supposed to help Mary find her love and move on. What happened?"

"I don't know. Maybe the black thing that was inside her is holding her there."

I shook my head. "The black thing isn't *in* her anymore. I would have been able to see it."

"You didn't see it before," Andy countered.

"Because I wasn't looking for it. Now that I know what it looks like, *feels* like, I would have known if it was inside her again."

"Then, why else would she be trapped here?"

The way he said *trapped* made my breath catch. "I don't know."

"I'm going to do some research tonight. We'll figure this out," Tristan offered.

We pulled into my driveway and Andy pulled up to the back porch. He turned off the truck and sat for a minute. "Your dad's not home. You want us to stay for a while?"

"I'm fine, really. I think it would do me some good to be alone tonight."

Tristan shot Andy a look.

"Would you stop that?" I said, my voice coming out angrier than I intended. "Sorry. I... you guys have been looking at each other like that a lot when I'm around. You can tell me if you think I'm going crazy."

Andy laughed. "Of *course,* we'd tell you if you were going crazy, Anderson. In fact, I'd be the first to tell you." He got out of the truck and leaned on the side of the bed, looking across at me. "We are worried about you. We have been since everything happened at the bridge. Everything that happened..."

"...and happens," Tristan said, getting out and standing next to Andy.

"...seems to happen to you worse than everyone else. We're worried about how much you can take."

I stood up straight. *You have no idea how much I can take.* "I am a strong person and I've had my whole life to learn to deal with seeing ghosts. I'm learning to deal with my mom's death, and I'm learning how to deal with my friend possibly dying. I don't need your sympathy or your worry. I need your friendship and I need your help helping ghosts."

Andy smiled. "That's what I wanted to hear. I think what we're doing is a good thing. We helped Old Man Dietrich and Kristen's family and Amalie's. We're doing good things here and I don't want one little setback to discourage you."

"It feels like more than a little setback," I mumbled.

"We'll figure it out," Tristan said, "but tonight, there is nothing more we can do. Tonight, we need to focus on getting ready to help Evie. Because she's going to need all of our help to get through this."

I snorted and half-smiled. "I'm glad I have you both," I said.

Andy rolled his eyes. "We're a package deal with the Eve-ster."

"No, seriously, just because we're close doesn't mean I am any less your friend than hers. I love you both," I said, surprised with the warmth that flooding through me, and the genuineness of the comment.

"We're going to go before this gets weird." Andy smiled.

"'Night, Marissa. We'll see you tomorrow first thing at the hospital."

I waved as Tristan got in the car and then I climbed the steps.

"Anderson!" Andy called.

I turned around.

"We love you, too, you big sap."

I headed into the house, locking the door behind me. I went through the house, flipping on lights as I went. Turning on the news, I made tomato soup and grilled cheese. My phone buzzed on the table. Dad was headed home. I ate, the warm soup coating my insides. I finished the last drop as Dad pulled into the driveway. He came up the steps and into the kitchen.

"Hey," I said, rinsing out my bowl.

"Hey, yourself." He stopped and looked at me. "Worried?"

"Yeah."

"Me, too."

"Any change?"

He sat down heavily at the table and ran his hands through his hair. "No, she's not doing very well."

I sighed. "You want me to fix you something to eat?"

"I'm good. I ate on the way home. You going to bed?"

I nodded. "Yeah, I'm tired."

"Night, Peanut."

"Night, Dad."

I climbed the stairs and headed into the bathroom to take a shower. When I came out, I put on my fluffy pajamas and turned off the light. I got into bed and pulled my phone over. The blue light on top was flashing. I pulled up the messages.

Kristen had texted me. I opened the text and almost dropped my phone. There was a photo of Hilda sitting on Hannah's nightstand. The text read; *I gave you the doll when you left my house. Why is it back???*

I stared at the picture. Then, I put it into its own window and zoomed in. On the bottom of the dress was snow. I put my hand over my mouth. *What was going on?*

I texted her and let her know that I'd be out the next day to talk. She texted back that her husband would be in town until after the New Year. I wasn't to come before then.

I took a screenshot of the conversation and sent it to Andy and Tristan, and as an afterthought, I texted it to

Evie as well. She would be able to help when she was back in her body, right? Laying my head on my pillow, I felt exhaustion take hold. My eyes closed and I slept.

That night, I dreamed that I was running through the forest by Mary's house. I came upon a clearing and Mary was standing there, Old Man Dietrich in a chair at her side. The doll sat on his lap and Amalie sat shivering in the moonlight. *Why won't you help us?* Their collective voices said. I fell to my knees in front of them, guilt washing over me. *I tried.* A moment later, Evie walked out from behind a tree. The gash on her forehead was unbandaged and blood ran down her face into her eyes. She looked at me and reached out for me. *Help me, Marissssa!*

I sat upright in bed, my pillow wet with tears. The windows were pink with the promise of dawn. I threw the comforter from my legs and got up, wrapping my robe around me as I walked to the door. I could hear Dad downstairs in the kitchen. The familiar sounds of him making coffee and rustling the paper calmed my frayed nerves. I got ready and met him downstairs.

"You're up early."

"I want to go with you to the hospital."

He furrowed his brow. "This might be a rough one today."

"I want to be there."

"You *should* be there, in case," he stopped talking and poured a cup of coffee into his travel mug. "Ready?"

I nodded emphatically and followed him out the door, away from the pleading voices in my dream.

We got into his truck and he started it, letting it warm up and clear the frost from the windows. He rubbed his hands together, making a sound like sandpaper in the quiet truck. "You seem upset. Is it Genevieve?"

I nodded, looking down at my hands in my lap. "So, she thinks she knows how to get back to her body today," I said, waiting for my dad's reaction.

"Hmmm," he said.

"She told me that she should be back by this morning."

He reached over and placed a hand on my shoulder. "We're going with that this morning because I don't want to think about the alternative."

I looked out of the side of my eye at my dad. He usually met things head on. I wasn't used to him avoiding thinking or talking about things. It made it even more real how scared he was that we were going to lose Evie.

The rest of the drive was quiet and we made our way up to her room. The doctor was in the room when we arrived. "We're going to need to get her father in here. He is going to have to sign some papers," the doctor said. He noted my dad's face and set jaw, and then said, "He is her father and we need to have the DNR on file."

"What's a DNR?" I asked in a small voice.

Dad pressed his lips together. "It's a Do Not Resuscitate order," he replied.

My heart thumped uncomfortably in my chest. The end was near and I could feel it in my core.

I sat down in the chair and listened to my dad and the doctor talk. Their words didn't come through, only a droning sound.

We waited at her bedside for an hour. I sat in the chair next to my dad in the hospital room. Nothing. *Maybe things are taking longer than they anticipated.* I tried to quell the feeling of dread that was creeping from my stomach into my chest.

Dad left to get some coffee and Andy and Tristan knocked on the door a little later and came in. "Patton awake yet?"

"Not yet," I said.

We talked about the plan and wondered together why it was taking so long.

The silence hung between us as we watched our friend wasting away on the hospital bed. I didn't know when the sadness would come. With my mom, it came in waves as I walked past her hospital bed in our living room every day. It would ebb when I went to school but hit me full force as I walked up the front steps of our house in St. Louis. *Why aren't you sad about Evie? Why aren't you crying? Why aren't you acting* normal*?* I sat with my questions for a moment, knowing the answer almost before I realized it. I wasn't mourning for Evie because I didn't believe that she would really die. She was going to get better and she was going to wake up and go back to being a giant pain in the rear end. We would have fights and laugh, and sit up until ungodly hours of the night watching reruns of *The Gilmore Girls*. She wasn't going anywhere.

Andy cleared his throat, jolting me back to the hospital room.

"What?"

"I asked you what you think happened with the doll," he said. "Why it came back."

I bit my bottom lip. "We didn't help Amalie either."

"You think she's at the house, too?"

I nodded then sighed. "Something is keeping the spirits from moving on." I wished for a moment that I could ask Evie what was going on - as if she had the inside track to this information. I looked down at her still face and flinched before I looked away. "Kristen said her husband would be home until after the New Year, so we weren't welcome before that. Her text sounded pretty angry."

"Remember what Evie said about Old Man Dietrich?" Tristan asked. His tone was gentle.

"Sometimes fear comes across as anger. She's afraid. She's scared for her little girl."

I nodded. "I get that. I wish we could help her. I wish we could help all of them." I felt Andy's eyes on me. "And, I know that you told me that I can't save them all, but I can. *We* can. We just have to figure out how."

Dad came back into the room. "I need to go get Genevieve's father. I'm going to head out soon and pick him up."

"Are you going to let him sign the paper?"

Dad sighed and ran his hand through his hair. "I don't have a choice. He's still her father and until he signs over his parental rights, he has final say over this." He stood quietly, considering Evie for a moment. "Where is she?" he asked.

I pressed my lips together. "I don't know. She said that she figured out how to get back to her body." I sighed. "She was supposed to be back by today."

Dad nodded his head, pulling a butterscotch candy from his pocket. "Well, the day is still early. Don't give up hope, honey." He patted my shoulder. "I'll be right back."

I excused myself and began pacing the hallway after Dad left, running through what I should do. *Make a plan, Marissa. Make a plan so that you know when to act. Fine,* I told myself, *a plan. If Evie doesn't come back to her body by four, I'm going to go to the City*

Hall and try to find Sam and Evie. If they can't get Evie back into her body, then I at least need to help her get here so that she can recharge.

When Dad got back to the room, it was nearly two in the afternoon and there had been no change in the state of Evie's body.

Andy, Tristan, and I looked up as he came in.

I squinted. "Where's her dad?"

"Come out here and talk to me for a minute."

I looked at the boys. Andy shrugged. Then, I followed Dad out into the hallway. "What's wrong? Why were you gone so long?"

Dad sat down in one of the plastic covered chairs in the hallway. He patted the seat of the one next to him and looked up at me.

Something's wrong. I bit back the feeling of dread as I walked over and sat down. "What's going on?"

Dad pulled a sheet of paper out of his pocket. "Genevieve's father was gone by the time I got to the hotel."

"I don't understand. Where did he go?"

"I assume back to Austin."

The words hit me right in the middle of the gut and I felt like the wind had been knocked out of me. *"Austin?"*

A nurse at the counter looked up at me then back down at the paperwork she was working on.

I lowered my voice a notch. "What happened? He's supposed to be here. *For Evie!"*

My dad closed his eyes and then opened them and fixed me with a calm gaze. "He left this." He passed me the sheet of paper.

I looked hard at it. "This is," I looked up at my dad then back down. "this is the paperwork to sign over his rights as a parent. It's the same thing her mother signed." My core trembled and I shook my head. "No, no, no, she can't go through this." My voice hitched with all the emotion that was bubbling up from my middle. "She can't handle this."

"We have two options," Dad said. "We can one, tell her what happened and help her process, or two, we can keep her father's visit a secret." He considered my face for a moment. "Which, if I am to read your countenance appropriately, will not be an option because she already knows her father was here. Did she meet him?"

I nodded. "Sorry," I mumbled.

"It's okay. It was a terrible option. I wouldn't want to lie to her." He took the paper from me and folded it, sliding it back in his shirt pocket and then sitting back in the chair. He rested his head against the wall and rolled it over to look at me. "She'll be able to handle this, honey. She has been able to handle everything that's ever been thrown at her, both figuratively and literally. She's strong."

"Who are you trying to convince?" My tone was quiet and my heart was aching with the thought of having to explain to Evie that she'd been left. Again.

Dad patted my knee as he stood up. "Let's get back in there. We want to be there when she comes back."

I sat for a moment as Dad walked to the door. "Who has to sign the DNR now?"

His hand froze on the doorknob and he dropped his head. Pressing his lips together, he opened the door and disappeared through it.

I sat for another few minutes in the chair, my mind spinning and my stomach churning. I closed my eyes and put every fiber in my being into concentrating on getting Evie back today. Sam needed to know what he was doing and she had to come back. Today. I didn't want to think of the consequences if she didn't.

When I got back into the room, Dad, Andy and Tristan were sitting in chairs around the bed, each looking at their phones. Evie hadn't moved. I sat down on the edge of the bed and watched her. For hours. I watched her while Dad left to get coffee. I watched her while Andy and Tristan went downstairs to get something to eat. I watched her as the afternoon rays of sun spread their buttery fingers out over the tree limbs outside the window. By four in the afternoon, nothing had happened. She hadn't woken up. She hadn't even moved. Anger spread through me. *Sam lied to her. He didn't know how to fix her, and now she was with him instead of recharging with her body.*

"I have to go," I said.

Dad looked up at me. "Where?"

"I have to check on something. I'll be back later."

He gave me a look that told me everything I needed to know so I nodded and I looked over at Andy and Tristan. They followed me as I walked down the steps and out into the cold air. Andy drove me over to City Hall and parked his truck.

CHAPTER 21

"What's next, Anderson?"

I stood staring up at the City Hall in the middle of the square. "Where is she, Sam?" I yelled. "Why didn't you help her?"

Andy and Tristan came up on either side of me. "Um, maybe we don't stand outside and yell at a building. You're drawing a crowd." He tried to take my arm, but I shook him off and climbed the stairs to the double doors. The lobby was dim and people were busy locking up their doors for the day. We walked past them to the circular stairs and started up.

"Can I help you?" The same girl sat at the information desk.

"Um, no thanks," I said, still climbing the stairs.

"I can't let you go up there," she said, chewing on a huge blob of gum. "We're closing."

"We'll just be a minute," I said over my shoulder.

Andy and Tristan hesitated for a moment, but when the bored girl shrugged and continued playing solitaire on her computer, they followed me up the stairs.

At the restrooms, I went around the corner and pressed my face to the door. "Evie! Sam! Are you there?" I reached for any bit of feeling that they were in the room above. Nothing. I turned around and shook my head at Andy and Tristan. "They're not here."

"Where else would they be? Can Sam leave the courthouse?" Tristan asked.

Realization dawned on me. Sam *had* to be here. He couldn't go anywhere else. I leaned into the door again. "Sam, it's Marissa. Open the door and talk to me, please?"

We stood there for a long time, waiting for any sign of Sam or Evie. I tried the door every few minutes, but it remained locked.

As the lights dimmed on the second floor, a security guard passed by the corridor. Andy, Tristan, and I attempted to fit our three bodies into a space that could barely fit one.

"We're closing. Time to go," the guard said.

"Excuse me, sir, would it be possible to get upstairs for a minute?" I asked.

Tristan jumped in, pulling out his phone and smiling at the guard. "We're working on a paper at school about the architecture of this building and we wanted to take a few photos of the third floor structure." He smiled winningly. "I'm using it for my entrance essay for LSU next year."

"Geaux, Tigers," the guard smiled. "My wife went there for her undergrad. I'm a Mizzou fan myself, but there's no accounting for taste."

"Bet that makes for some interesting football Saturdays in your house," Tristan said. "Since their entry into the SEC a few years ago, right?"

The guard smiled again. He pulled out a set of keys from his pocket. "I guess it wouldn't hurt to let you take a few pictures."

We stepped aside and I shot a bewildered glance in Tristan's direction. He waggled his eyebrows at me and smiled.

"This structure was completed in 1905. This was the last thing they completed, well, aside from hanging the chandelier." The guard continued his running commentary as we climbed, Tristan diligently writing notes in his notepad and asking questions of the guard as they walked. Upstairs, I went immediately to the circular window where Sam stayed. The area looked and felt empty. *He's not here, and neither is Evie.* I looked over at Tristan, who was taking photos with his phone and shook my head.

"I want to thank you so much for allowing us up here. It will really help my report."

"I'd like to read it when you're done," the guard said as he ushered us downstairs, locking the door behind him.

"I'll mention you in the footnotes," Tristan said. After writing down the guard's name, Tristan turned to me. "See, I told you that the attic was the only place that was barred from public access."

"Well, that's not exactly true," the guard said. "Did you do some research on the basement?"

Tristan widened his eyes. "No, I didn't even know there was a basement in this place. It's not on any of the plans I could find online."

The guard snorted. "Yeah, they blocked it off back in the nineties. Come on, I'll show you." He seemed to be happy to be talking to someone. I imagined being the night guard would be lonely.

He led us down the stairs and to the back of the building. As we walked along the corridor, my stomach started to turn and the blood in my arms and legs turned to ice. Whispers passed along the hallway above my head, bouncing off the ceiling and moving past my head.

I couldn't pick out what they were saying, but the tone was ominous.

The guard took out his keys again and unlocked the basement door. He reached in and waved an arm into the stale air that had been trapped behind the locked door. A stench reached my nostrils and I reached up to hold a hand over my nose and mouth. Andy looked over at me and I nodded. Somewhere, down below, were Sam and Evie.

Sam! Evie! I tried to reach out to them in the only way I knew how. *Evie!*

Nothing.

"Is there another way into the basement?" Tristan asked, snapping a few photos of the concrete barrier.

The guard shook his head. "This was the only entrance into the basement that was built. There are supposed to be holding cells and a well down there, but when the city put in the sewer system, it was decommissioned." He launched into the story of the city councilwoman's daughter and I took the opportunity to move a little way down the hallway.

Andy followed me. "Are they down there?" he whispered.

I nodded. "They can't hear me, though. Andy, I need to get out of here, *soon.*"

"I've got you," he said. Then, louder, "Come on, man. I have to pick up my little sister from band practice. Mom will kill me if I forget again."

Thankfully, Tristan took the hint. "Well, thank you so much for your time. I really appreciate it."

"No worries, I'll show you out," the guard said.

He locked the basement door and walked us down the corridor to the front lobby. He unlocked the front doors and held the left one open for us. "Nice to meet you guys. Let me know if you need any more information about the place. I'm here most nights."

"Thanks again," Tristan waved as he led the way down the steps.

"Oh, I almost forgot," the guard said.

We turned.

"There's supposedly a cave that leads into the basement. Two inmates disappeared from their holding cells down there in the thirties and they were never heard from again. Rumor has it they escaped into the cave and died there. No official record of that, though," he said. "Night, guys." He closed the door behind him.

Andy, Tristan and I stood there for a long minute, no one saying anything. Then we all started talking at once.

"We have to get to Sam and Evie."

"Where do you think the cave starts?"

"Could we get in there?"

"We're going to try to talk to Sam on the Ouija board."

"I'm going to need about three cheeseburgers before we do that."

***

At my house later, Andy and Tristan were seated in my room on the floor. My dad had been home but left again for the hospital. I was glad someone would be there to watch over Evie's body. After I filled the boys in on what I saw when Jeff was there, neither one of them wanted to leave Evie alone.

"I don't think it's safe," Andy said.

"It's so cute when you play protective," Tristan teased.

"I could totally protect her," he said, feigning hurt.

"Of course, you could."

"Well, until we figure out what that black mist is, I think it's a good idea that someone stay with Evie's body all the time," I said.

The boys agreed.

I placed the board on the floor and sat down next to them. Seeing the board made me think of Evie and thinking of Evie made my heart hurt. I shook my head to get rid of the feeling. I couldn't help her if I let my emotions get in the way.

We placed our fingers on the planchette and I closed my eyes. "Sam, Sam, please come talk to us. We need to know where Evie is." I waited, my eyes closed to feel my fingers moving at all. When they didn't, I opened my eyes and looked at Andy and Tristan. "Nothing."

"Keep trying," Tristan said.

"Sam, Sam, please come talk to us," I said. I concentrated my whole being on reaching out to Sam. A moment later, the room seemed to spin on its axis. "Something's happening," I whispered. The planchette started moving and I looked down. It swung in a slow circle and then up to the H. It was followed by E, R, E. I sat back on my knees and looked over at Andy. "Sam, is that you?"

YES.

"Is Evie with you?"

NO, then, YES.

"What happened? Why didn't she come back to her body?"

The planchette moved, slowly at first and then faster. NEED HELP.

"Where are you?" I asked. My hands were suddenly clammy. I removed them and wiped them on my jeans before placing them back.

The board stayed still for several minutes.

"Did we lose him?" Andy asked.

I shook my head. "No, I think he's still here. He feels…conflicted. No, that's not right either. It feels like he's hiding something." Then, louder, "Sam, Evie's body is dying. She doesn't have very long. You have to get her back to her body soon. Do you understand?"

The planchette swung up to YES and stayed there, trembling over the word.

"We can help you, but we can't get to the basement in the courthouse."

FLUTE.

Flute? What does that mean? Then, I realized exactly what he meant. "He's speaking in code. Someone must be near that he doesn't want to know."

Andy shook his head. "Who?"

"I don't know." I leaned over the board. "Sam, I know where that is. Do you want us to come now?"

The planchette swung around in our hands, whipping itself away from our fingertips and spinning over the word YES. A moment later, it stopped and the feeling was gone. I sat back and looked over at Andy and Tristan. I felt the color drain from my face. *I don't want to go back there.*

"What did he mean when he said flute?" Tristan asked. He boxed up the Ouija board and held it on his lap as he sat cross-legged on the floor.

I got up to sit down on my bed and Andy hit the futon. "Right after Thanksgiving, Evie told me she wanted to go on a walk in the cold and snow. Anyway, we went out and she showed me a cave on the back of our property. We went in and that's when I saw the vision of the tribe of Native Americans sitting and dancing around a fire in the cave."

"You drew a picture of what you saw."

I nodded. "Yeah, it was the first time I'd ever drawn anything like that. But, what I didn't tell you guys was that Evie called the vision."

Tristan cocked his head to the side. "She *called* your vision?"

"I think so. She used her phone to play some flute music. As soon as it started playing, I began to see into the past."

"How did Sam know about the flute music?"

Andy shrugged. "Maybe Patton told him?"

I pressed my lips together. "I don't think so. I mean, if they were communicating through the Ouija board, why would she waste that much effort on telling him about the flute music? She might tell him about the drawing, or me seeing something, but until recently, their entire relationship took place through the medium of broken sentences and words here and there."

Tristan nodded. "Do you think he was there?"

I spun the idea around in my mind. "I don't think so. Ghosts are tied to the land where they died or where their body is buried."

"Evie can move around anywhere she wants," Tristan said.

"She's not really a ghost. She's a soul without a body." I glared at Andy as he opened his mouth to say something. "There's a difference."

"But ghosts, *real* ghosts can't leave the land they died on?"

"Right. Sam died at the courthouse and I don't think he's buried anywhere near here, so I don't think it was him."

Andy sat up. "What if the land where they died has a cave system underneath it?"

"What do you mean?"

"Well, if what the guard said was true, then there *could* be a cave system running from under the courthouse to the cave you and Evie were in. He could have seen you then."

I considered Andy for a moment. "Maybe." Something felt unsettling about the whole thing but I couldn't quite put my finger on what was wrong. I sighed and stood up. "We need to get going." I got out my phone and let my dad know that something came up, and that we were going to try to help Evie. His response was almost immediate. *Be careful.*

Andy and Tristan texted their parents while I pulled my boots out of my closet. I yanked on the laces and pulled on another sweatshirt. Downstairs, we gathered coats, flashlights, some bungee cords and a couple of emergency flares.

Andy looked at me while I held them in my hands, considering. "I don't think we're going to need those." Then, he cocked his head to the side. "You know, I'm not exactly sure what we need to do this."

Tristan took his cue and brought his phone out. A couple minutes of scrolling later, he found a site and started reading off a supply list: "Headlamps, first aid kit, reflective tape to mark the way, extra flashlights, rope..."

Andy and I pulled things from the shelves in the mudroom while Tristan listed them. My dad only owned a couple of headlamps, but he had a box full of flashlights. We packed Tristan's and my backpacks with supplies and Andy packed his with recording equipment.

"This isn't an investigation," I reminded him. "This is a rescue mission. We have to get to Evie and get her back to her body before it's too late."

"We want to remember this, though," he argued.

I'm not so sure I want to.

We headed out and I locked up behind us. I left the lights in the kitchen and on the back porch blazing into the cold night as we trudged away through the woods. I tried to remember exactly where Evie led me, but had to keep turning back to get my bearings by the lights. When we traveled far enough into the woods that I could no longer see the house, I relied on memory alone. Andy and Tristan followed me quietly, allowing me to navigate without interruption. I found the path without too much trouble and we wound our way down to the small creek. It snaked along, a trickling sound underneath a clear sheet of thin ice. The mirror-like surface reflected the moon's rays and tossed them back at jaunty angles throughout the forest.

"It's over here," I said over my shoulder. *I think.*

We moved along the gully and I almost missed the mouth of the cave, hidden as it was behind an outcropping of rocks and dead underbrush. I moved some of the dry leaves with my foot and there was the entrance, a large hole near the bank of the creek.

"Here it is."

"Nice job, Anderson."

"Thanks." I felt my cheeks flush with the compliment.

I was the first into the opening and I slid into the large room, landing on my rear end in an unceremonious jumble. Tristan alit beside me, impeccable in his blue down coat and red scarf and hat. He extended a gloved hand and I took it, pulling myself up onto my feet.

Andy came through next, twisting his long, lanky frame to make it fit through the unforgiving space. When he got inside, he turned and pulled his backpack in and strapped it to his back as he stood up. "What now?" he asked, his voice echoing in the cavernous space.

I struggled out of my warm coat and tossed it, along with my hat and scarf, on a rock. Here in the cave, it was cool, but much warmer than outside and our windbreakers were sufficient. Tristan and Andy followed suit and left their heavy coats lying in a pile on top of mine near the entrance. I bent down and unzipped my backpack. Reaching in, I pulled out three flashlights. "Here, take one so we'll all have an extra." I stood there, uncertain. "I don't know what to do next."

"Do you have to do something special to see Sam?" Tristan asked. He shined his light around the giant room.

I shook my head. "No, I've always been able to see him without doing much of anything. I need to concentrate."

Tristan and Andy stood together near the entrance while I walked around the space, running my gloved hand along the smooth limestone.

"Sam, are you here?" My question echoed along the walls. My headlamp flashed over the pictures scratched into the wall and Tristan stepped forward and snapped a picture of them with his phone. I walked around the room twice before coming back to the entrance and standing next to the boys.

"Anything?" Andy asked.

I shook my head. "I don't understand. I thought for sure this was the place." I rubbed a hand over my tired eyes. The stress of the past week was beginning to catch up with me and I leaned my head to the left, allowing the tight muscles to stretch. As I was leaning my head to the right, a strange feeling came over me. A mixture of dizziness and lightheadedness wound around me and I reached out to hold onto Tristan's arm.

"Is he here?"

I nodded. "No, but I think something's happening."

Chattering, like a hundred people talking all at once spread around the room. I tilted my head, trying to follow one line of conversation but failing. A warm orange light spread out from a crack in the wall near the pictures. The glowing grew more intense and I took a step back as a shadow spread on the wall.

"Someone's coming," I whispered.

"We don't see anything," Andy said.

"There's a glow and a shadow. Over there." I pointed.

The shadow lengthened, spreading across the wall opposite. I held my breath as a figure appeared from the back of the rock. An antique lantern came out first, held by an arm attached to a dark figure. I squinted, looking closely. The figure seemed to be shrouded in darkness that the lantern's light didn't penetrate. He turned his face and the light sizzled and went out. I fumbled to turn

on my headlamp and when I did, the entire room was splashed in the bright LED. The figure turned to me and smiled.

"You came," he said, striding over to me. "Thank you so much."

"It's Sam," I told Andy and Tristan. I spun around and looked at Sam. "Where's Evie?"

The smile faded. He looked down at the ground and then back up at me. "Evie's in trouble."

THE DEVIL DOLL

CHAPTER 22

"I know she's in trouble! She has to get back in her body or it's going to die and she's going to get stuck here forever!" Anger poured out of me, directed straight at Sam.

He hung his head again. "I know. I thought I could help her. I did everything he said to do." His gaze lifted and met mine. "I'm sorry."

A cold ball of worry spun around in my stomach. "Sam," I spoke slowly, "where is Evie?"

"We don't have a lot of time. We can talk while we walk."

I nodded to the guys. "We have to get going. Grab your backpacks." I pulled mine onto my shoulders and followed Sam to the crack in the wall. He disappeared inside and the orange glow flashed onto the walls.

Andy grabbed my shoulder as I was about to duck into the small space. "Are you sure this is safe, Anderson?"

I'm not. Everything inside me is telling me to turn around. "It's fine. We'll be fine." I turned and followed Sam.

He led us down into a long tunnel. Tributaries spread out to the side and I shined my flashlight down each one, my eyes searching for the end to the darkness but not finding one.

"Are you sure you know where you're going?" I asked, squeezing myself through a particularly small space.

Sam stopped on the other side and turned around to hold the lantern up for me as I made my way through. On the other side of the small space was a larger room, spreading out into a huge arching ceiling.

I went to Mark Twain Cave in Hannibal, Missouri with my parents when I was younger, and I remembered how thrilling it was when the guides brought everyone into a room and told us to hold on to something before they turned off all the lights. I remembered not being able to see my hand in front of my face and the sensation of my stomach jumping at the all-encompassing darkness. Then, the lights were turned back on and the entire cave was flooded in a warm yellowish-orange glow and the tour continued. Here, though, our lamps only created pinpricks of light and the darkness spread around us, pressing down with an almost physical presence. I could *feel* the darkness and wrapped my fingers around the additional flashlight in my pocket. *If the lights go out in here, we're lost.* The enormity of the situation threatened to overwhelm me, and I gulped down a few gulps of cool air as Andy and Tristan came through the space behind me.

Tristan looked at me and I couldn't hide the tears that sprang to my eyes.

"Sam, hold up. Marissa needs a minute." He pulled a bottle of water from his bag and handed it to me. "Did he hear me?"

I looked over and saw Sam standing near the end of the room. "Yeah, um, thanks." I squatted down, taking a long drink of water from the bottle. "I got scared."

The sound of tearing tape reached my ears and I looked over to see Andy spreading a reflective arrow near the place where we entered.

"We have to be able to find our way out again." He shrugged.

My skin crawled. There were a million ways to die that I was scared to death of. Wandering around underground until my light ran out and I died was among the top ten, right behind drowning and burning up in a fire. I shook my head to clear it. "Sam, can you please tell me what happened?"

He walked over and considered me with gentle eyes. "After I spoke with the old spirit about how to get Evie back into her body, the spirit said that he wanted to meet her. To see what a wandering soul looked like."

"And you took her? Knowing how little time she had left?"

"H-he told me that he would show me how I died."

"I was going to help you!" My voice barely hid the exasperation I felt.

"You weren't able to get into the basement of the courthouse." Sam looked at me.

Realization poured over me. "And you were afraid that once Evie got back in her body, we would all forget about you."

"I haven't had anyone to talk to for such a long time." His voice held such a sense of sadness.

I sat there, torn between not trusting Sam and having to trust him to save my best friend. My head hurt and I gulped down the rest of the water. I stood up then and put the empty bottle in my bag. "Let's go."

"I'm sorry, Marissa." Sam peered at me above the circle of orange light.

"How much farther?"

Sam nodded. "The center of town is about five miles from your house by road. The cave system leads directly into it though, so we've got about two and a half miles to go."

I relayed the message to Andy and Tristan and we set off. The going was relatively easy, but my legs were soon burning from the effort of walking on uneven surfaces. I could hear Andy and Tristan walking behind me and the sound was comforting. *Should I tell them about my reservations about Sam? Would it make a difference?* I decided it wouldn't. They were with me for the long haul, following me down into the bowels of the earth based on my ability to see a ghost. I felt honored and frightened all at once.

About two hours later, Sam slowed.

"Are we close?"

He stood for a moment and looked up at the ceilings that towered out of sight above. "Yes, we're close. We're underneath Main Street now." He stood at a fork. "That way leads out to the quarry and this way goes to the middle of town." He started walking again to the fork on the right.

"How do you know your way around in here so well?" I asked, noting the rise to the footing below. We were climbing. "Tristan tried to look it up and there's only one part of this cave that's mapped and that's all the way out by the quarry."

"Most of the cave system is untouched. It spreads out like a wagon wheel underneath the town and City Hall is the hub. Not many people know about it because there are only a few entrances: one on your farm, one by the quarry, and the fabled one in the basement of the courthouse."

"Is that one real?" I asked.

"After I died, I don't know how long it was before I started hearing stories about the cave system below here. I searched until I found a hole carved into the wall of one of the holding cells in the basement of the courthouse."

"From the inmates who broke out?"

"Yes, their names were Andrew Cunningham and Trent Sampson. Two boys from Texas. They were robbing banks all along the northern road from Texas through Oklahoma and Arkansas before the law finally caught up with them in Missouri. They were awaiting extradition to Texas when they disappeared from the holding cells. The police sent a search party, but they turned back long before they found them."

I tripped on a rock and Tristan steadied me from behind. "They made it out?"

Sam glanced behind, the side of his face illuminated in the light from the lantern. "No." He walked a few more steps before saying more. "I started exploring the caves and found them, or what was left of them, in a cave that stretched out into the west side of town. They were only about forty yards from an entrance."

"Oh." I didn't know what else to say so I stayed quiet.

As we walked, the air began to get thicker and smelled worse. I assumed we were under a sewer system, but wasn't sure and didn't want Andy to call me "City" again, so I stayed quiet. At some point, I realized that the space had gotten narrower. The floor angled sharply up and then stopped before we nearly tumbled out into an open space.

"Careful here," Sam warned.

I caught myself before losing my footing on the wet rocks. My flashlight caught the smooth surface spreading out like glass as far as my light reached. Ripples spread out from where my foot touched the edge, catching the light and playing it across the water and up onto the ceiling and walls. I backed up a bit. "Be careful, there's water up here."

Sam stood a few feet away, clinging to the wall with one hand and his lantern with the other. "This is the lake that used to supply the water to the town."

"How far down are we?" Tristan asked from behind me.

"I don't know. Sam?"

He looked up, squinting into the darkness. "I'd say about a hundred and twenty feet down."

I relayed the message and heard a groan behind me.

"How on earth are we going to get up there?"

"He's gotten us this far," I said, "so trust him a little longer."

Sam edged around the lake and we followed suit, gliding our backs along the wet walls. It pressed in on me and I tried to breathe and *not* think about the one hundred twenty feet of dirt and concrete hanging above my head. I slipped once and my foot plunked into the water. Tristan grabbed my shoulder to steady me and we continued. On the other side, a walkway sloped up for a long way and then it opened up into a small cavern. We stopped to catch our breath and regroup.

Sam held his lamp up and illuminated a small hole in the wall of the cavern. "This is it."

I shined my flashlight and then knelt down and looked at the hole. "You're kidding me, right?"

Sam shook his head. "I'm afraid not. It's only small like this for about ten feet and then it widens again before we get to the basement. It will be fine."

"He says that it's only small for about ten feet." I tried to imagine what it would feel like to have the walls of the cave pressing in on me on all sides and I felt my heartbeat begin to race. I took a couple of deep breaths. "We have to get to Evie."

Tristan came into my flashlight beam and looked at me. "If you're scared, you can stay here and Andy and I can go."

I considered it for a nanosecond, but then shook my head. "I need to be there. She would do it for me."

Tristan nodded, his eyes still on me. "We'll be with you the entire time."

I took a deep breath and got down on my hands and knees, my head sticking into the hole. I nodded to Sam. "Let's go."

He got down on his hands and knees and started into the hole, army crawling his way in. I took a deep breath and followed his feet. The flashlight I held in my mouth, my teeth chattering around it. The floor was slippery and cold and the walls pressed in on my back and shoulders. I heard Tristan shuffling through behind me with his wide shoulders. I could imagine Andy struggling to push his long frame through the small space. The lantern Sam carried clanged every time he placed it on the floor a few feet ahead and then crawled to it. I could see a little of its light as a halo around his body. It was slow going and my elbows and knees throbbed. I tried to count the feet as we went.

"You okay up there?" Tristan panted.

"Yeah." The passage seemed to go on forever and I was so tired. It didn't help that the entire thing sloped up, so we were not only fighting against the small space, but also the climb.

After what seemed like an eternity, Sam's feet disappeared and his face reappeared in a hole.

"You're almost there," he said.

I pushed my body along the last few feet through pure determination and then I was out, too. I turned to help Tristan and then Andy. Andy slumped over, his breathing labored. Tristan offered him some water and stood watchful.

I took a moment to look around this space. It was wetter than the previous caverns and droplets of water hung in the air. The floor was covered in a fine layer of mud and my feet sunk down in it. "Where now?" I asked.

Sam pointed to the other wall. "That's the hole the inmates made."

I shined my flashlight over and saw crumbled concrete on the floor. The hole above the pile was small, and the darkness seemed deeper on the other side.

"We're here." I walked over and knelt down, steadying myself against the wall and shined the beam of light into the space. It was a small cell, walled in by large stones and concrete. "Evie!" I cried. My voice echoed and came back to me. *Eviiieeeee.* I felt the world around me shift and I caught myself before I fell into the darkness. "Evie, I'm coming!"

With that, I vaulted myself through the hole into the basement of the courthouse.

CHAPTER 23

Everything felt wrong the second I crossed into the basement. A horrid stench almost choked me and I put my sleeve up to my mouth, holding it against the retching. Tears filled my eyes and I stood up, trying to gulp down a fresh breath. I couldn't find one and my head felt swollen and cloudy.

Then, Andy was there holding me against his side for support. "What's wrong?"

I shook my head. "Everything," I managed to squeak out.

The odor spread up around me: death, misery, hopelessness. Beneath all of that was fear. And, a lot of it. I pushed away from Andy and went to the entrance of the cell. The bars were rusted and hanging askew from the stone frame. Tristan pushed them aside and I walked out into the basement of the courthouse. I shined the flashlight around, taking in my surroundings. It was a large open space. Lining the wall that we came through were a half dozen holding cells, most in complete disrepair and in the middle of the floor there was a circular stone well pushing up from the ground. Cobwebs clung to the rafters above me and I walked slowly toward the concrete-encased stairs. There was no one in the basement. *No Evie.* Everything inside me fell apart and the tears streamed down my face. I walked over to the well and peered down into the darkness.

"The well," Sam said as he came up alongside me. His gaze never left the surface.

I placed my hands on the cold stone. Immediately, I was transported back in time. *Sam, you're here.* I watched the Sam from the past walk over to the well and place his hands on the stones next to the ghost of Sam. Another man stood near him, helping to tie a rope around his middle. I watched as the first man lowered Sam over the side of the well.

Sam, what's wrong?

Sam's ghost took a sharp breath in. "I remember." He turned wide eyes in my direction. "I remember what happened to me now!" He reached out and took my hands as his past self disappeared into the well. "This man, um, Carter I believe was his name, was working with me down here and we were carving out the well. He lowered me down and I went as far as the rope would go, until the light at the top was only a small pinprick. I was lowered into a cavern. I *saw* something there."

"What did you see?" I felt Tristan and Andy close. They were right there in case something happened and with that feeling, my bravery grew.

Sam's eyes turned to the well. "I remember it hurt so badly. It felt like my entire body was being burned by hot irons."

"Sam, what happened in the well?"

He turned again to me, his gaze unwavering. "When I got down there, I saw someone. A-a man bathed in light and sitting cross legged on one end of the cavern. His face was calm, old, and wise. He was concentrating on something on the other side. I had to wait for the rope to spin me around, and when it did, I saw what he was focused on. It was the darkest thing I'd ever seen. It felt like evil." He shook his head. "I thought I saw a figure within all of that blackness, but I couldn't seem to make it out."

"When the rope spun me around again, the man in the light glanced at me, his concentration broken for a moment. He said one word to me." Sam paused and looked at me. "Gisa."

The word triggered something in my memory.

"A moment later, I was hit with a cloud of blackness that bit into my pores and speared itself into my very essence. It hurt like nothing I'd ever felt before and then, Carter was pulling me up. The blackness held onto me, fraying the rope as he pulled. As I got closer, he stopped to look down at me. His face twisted in horror and he started to back away, his mouth opening and closing as he started to pray."

I watched as Carter's eyes grew wide and he moved away. "Why is he doing that?"

The man's eyes filled with tears. "Y-you have the face of a demon!"

Sadness and fear washed over me. "What happened, Sam?"

Sam let go of my hands and placed them back on the stone.

A moment later, Carter's lips trembled. "God forgive me," he said as the rope slipped from his fingers. He struggled to pull the heavy cover onto the opening, looking down as he did so.

Sam's voice echoed from the darkness below: "Help me! Don't do this!"

"Forgive me," the man said and then pushed the cover into place. He ran up the stairs and out of the basement.

I whipped around and stared at Sam. "That's how you died?"

He nodded, tears filling his eyes. "He left me. He left me to die." Sam looked down at his hands, turning them this way and that. The light of the lantern sitting on the side of the well poured light onto his hands and I could see the skin ripped away from his fingertips. They were bloody and torn. He looked up at me, his eyes glinting in the light.

"How long did you hang on?" I asked, the words tearing at my throat. I leaned over the well and saw Sam clinging to the inside. He was praying, his voice catching in his throat as he cried two names over and over again, "Virginia. Sarah."

A moment later, his grip was lost and I turned away as he plummeted to the darkness below. Sam watched his figure and then finally turned away.

"Who are they? Virginia? Sarah?" I whispered.

He took a hitching breath. "My wife and daughter. Sarah was only a baby when I…" a sob cut him off, wrenching itself from his chest. Tears flowed freely down his cheeks and he sat down heavily, his back against the well. "I only saw her once more. She came here," he whispered, "when she got married. I got to see her when she came here. She was so happy, my little one." Sobs wracked his body again and he wiped at his eyes with his bloody hands, red streaks covering his face.

I knelt down beside him as the vision faded around me, the draining feeling spreading through my limbs. *I'm so sorry, Sam. Really, I am. I know what it's like to lose someone you love.* The feeling of loss pricked at me with icy fingers. I took a moment to fill in Tristan and Andy. They both extended their apologies, their faces drawn taut with worry.

"Sam, where's Evie?" I asked.

His sobs lessened and he sniffed loudly. "I came here to talk to the figure I saw, the old man filled with light. He is the oldest spirit I know. I stood here and talked to him. He told me what to do." He looked up at me. "I don't think it was him that wanted me to bring Evie here. When I brought her, she leaned over the edge of the well and something grabbed her. She was…gone!"

Oh, my God. Evie. The thought of my friend shook away the fogginess and my entire core shook as I used the edge of the stone to pull myself into a standing position. The stench returned and I could feel it wrapping around me, filling my lungs with putrid air. My hands were cold on the stone as I leaned over the edge, my tears falling into the pit below. "Evie?" I whispered. "Evie, are you here?"

I closed my eyes, willing her voice not to come up from the bottom of the well. Willing it to come from behind me. Not at all would have been better. I could pretend she was somewhere safe. Maybe she was already at the hospital back in her body.

All of my delusional hope was lost as a small voice wound its way up from the abyss below,

"Marissa, help me!"

My legs gave out and I hit the floor. "No, no, no."

Tristan was there, his hands on my upper arms, his face inches from mine. "She's down there?"

I nodded, hopelessness taking over my soul. *My best friend is trapped in the bottom of a well. And, it's all Sam's fault. If he hadn't brought her here, this never would have happened.* I shoved a cork in that line of thinking and closed my eyes, bringing my breath back to a normal pace and concentrating on building that feeling of safeness and love inside me. The feeling of my mother smoothing my hair back from my face. The feeling of my dad sitting in his office with his coffee. The feeling of Grant kissing me. The feeling of Evie and me laughing. The little ball of energy grew within me and I stood up, almost knocking Tristan back.

I walked over to my backpack and ripped the zipper open. I started rummaging through it, tossing flashlights and emergency kits out onto the floor.

"What are you doing?" Andy asked from behind me.

"I'm going down there."

"Um, that would be a hard no."

I turned around and looked up at him. "Evie is down there."

"I'll go down," he offered.

I pulled the roll of rope from the bag and stood up. I shook my head. "There's no way Tristan and I are strong enough to lower you down there."

"We could let Tristan go."

I shook my head again. "We might be able to get him down, but that's not the part I'm worried about. We wouldn't be able to pull him back up again. Sorry, Andy, this is the only way. I'm the smallest. It has to be me."

Andy set his jaw. "What if that thing happens to you when you see something, happens down there? We won't be able to get to you."

"It will be fine," I said with a confidence I didn't feel. "I'll be fine." I said again, hoping that a second time would make it true.

He looked at Tristan and widened his eyes.

"I don't see any other way."

"You're outvoted," I said. "Sam, where do I attach this?"

He directed me to attach the carabiner to a pipe near the well. I ran the rope through it and yanked down on it.

Andy grabbed the rope from my hands. "Have you ever done this before?"

I wished I could look up at him defiantly and indignant because he questioned my rock climbing abilities, but I was only able to raise my eyebrows and shrug. "I've seen videos."

Andy rolled his eyes and turned to Tristan. "Are we seriously going to let her do this?"

"She's not rock climbing. We only have to lower her down."

"And, I'll be with her the whole time," Sam said from his place near the well. He stood and placed his hand gently on my shoulder.

I shivered. "Sam will be with me the whole time."

"That's supposed to make me feel better?" Andy crossed his arms over his chest. "He doesn't exactly have the best record going down there."

I stood facing him. "Andy, we have to do this."

He blinked several times and then walked over. "What do I do?"

Sam told me how to make a harness in the end of the rope and I stepped into it. "You and Tristan keep tension on this length here. Lower me slowly, and when I get to the bottom tie it off. I'll yank twice when I want you to pull me up."

Andy still didn't look convinced.

"It's going to be okay, but if it's not…"

Tristan looked gray in the dim light.

I took a deep breath. "…and if something happens to me down there, get out and go get help. And, tell my dad that I love him."

I backed up to the well and let the backs of my legs rest against the stone. I pulled my knees up and put my legs into the darkness. I adjusted my headlamp and made sure two more flashlights were tucked into my pockets. I turned to look at Andy and Tristan. They held the rope in their hands, wrapped around several times, their feet braced against the side of the well.

"Here goes nothing." I gently slid my bottom off the edge and there was a sickening moment when I was free floating but then the rope caught and I was supported. The straps of the harness bit into my jeans, cutting off the circulation almost immediately. I gritted my teeth and nodded my head at my friends. "See you soon."

I watched their faces until I dipped below the edge of the well. Sam grabbed the rope a bit above me and held on as we were lowered down. I turned my headlamp down to illuminate the tunnel. I could barely hear the sound of the rope running over the edge for the blood beating through my ears. I took a deep breath and held onto the rope with both hands, squeezing my eyes shut as I began turning. I spiraled down through the well, the straps cutting into me every time Andy and Tristan jerked the rope. About halfway down, they found their rhythm and the ride became much smoother. The light began to reach out past the circular opening that was still thirty feet down. Then, twenty, ten, and five. As my feet entered the space below, I saw the cavern. I looked up at Sam. His face was grim. My head finally broke through to the room and then my feet touched solid ground.

"I'm down!" I shouted to the boys above and I felt the rope stop.

Sam let go and dropped, landing in a crouching position next to me. He stood, his mouth open wide and his eyes wider as a white light illuminated his features.

I spun around and came face to face with something from my nightmares.

CHAPTER 24

I cried out and took a step back. In front of me was Sam's lifeless body, lying twisted on the floor of the cavern. His eyes were turned up to the well and a hand was jutted out from his broken arm, forever reaching out to the light above.

Oh, Sam.

He stepped around me and walked to his body, peering down at it with a curious look on his face. I untangled myself from the harness and let it drop to the floor.

"Anderson?" Andy's voice sounded so far away.

"I'm down!" I shouted.

I watched Sam as he stood staring down at his body. He was silhouetted against a bright white light and I stepped around him for a better look.

Within the glow was a man. He was so bright it was hard to look at him directly.

I stepped closer. "Who are you?"

It is no matter who I am. What matters is who you are and what you are here for. It is afraid of you because you are the only one that can stop it.

I closed my eyes against the onslaught of light and cleared my mind. Warm feelings filled me and I almost smiled with the joy of the moment. "Are you a ghost?"

The man chuckled. *You could say that.*

"Marissa?" The voice was weak, but it was definitely Evie.

I opened my eyes and turned wildly around, trying to identify the source of her voice.

She's almost gone. There's not much time now.

"Evie!" I screamed into the darkness. I pulled my flashlights out of my pockets and began shining their beams wildly around the space. "Sam, help me find her!"

My voice shocked him out of his stupor and he was at my side.

"Where is she?" he asked the man.

There is great evil down here. It couldn't have you, but it will not stop until it has her. You were its first victim, Samuel, but not its last. It keeps them here. All of them.

My flashlight caught something moving in the shadows of the cavern. "Evie!" I cried out, stumbling my way across the slippery, uneven ground. My focus was laser-like as I moved across the great open space. I moved out of the light and the darkness fell over me, drowning out all of the happiness I ever felt. My mind numbed with the overwhelming feeling of sadness that poured into me. I let out a cry and fell to my knees, despair washing over me.

I looked up and saw Evie. She was standing near the back wall, her hair ragged and her clothing torn. Her eyes were haunted, deep-set with dark circles under them. "Marissa!" she called out through lips that were cracked and bleeding. She was so pale I could almost see through her. It tore at my heart and I started to cry.

Then Sam was there. He pulled me up and back into the light. I took a deep breath as warmth spread through me again, driving out the pain. "What was that?"

"The bad thing," Sam said, his eyes watchful.

"Evie's there," I moaned, "we have to help her."

Something shifted on that side of the cavern, a sloshing ugly sound like a thousand people crying out in pain all at once. My stomach churned. It was there. It knew I was there, and it wanted me.

There is only one way. You're the one it wants.

Something snapped within me and I knew what I had to do. She was my best friend.

I stood up straight then, my body calm and strong. I steeled myself against the sadness and the despair and continued to walk forward, my feet miring in the floor. I looked down and saw tendrils of blackness winding around my feet. They beckoned me forward, toward Evie and the darkness. I reached out for her, and as I did, the wisps met my hands, wrapping them in sadness, anger, fear. I gasped as they moved up my arms toward my face. I held my face back as the iciness wound around me. I was succumbing to it.

"I'm here," I said, my voice filling the cavern. "Let her go and take me instead."

With my words, the blackness tightened its grip on me, pulling me forward toward Evie. I felt lost, my body wasn't my own. I closed my eyes. I wondered if I would see my mother again.

I opened my eyes and locked gazes with Evie. She was crying. "No, Marissa," she mouthed.

I nodded. *It's okay.*

The darkness wrapped its arms around me and I allowed it. I felt my soul taken over by the darkness and I was wrapped in its icy embrace.

Suddenly, I felt arms behind me, gripping me solidly. I looked down and saw arms wrapped around me, filled with light.

"When I say run, you run. Do you understand?" Sam's voice whispered in my ear.

I shook my head. "No, it wants me."

"Not today," he whispered. His grip strengthened and he tensed. "Now!" he shouted. "Run!" He tossed me back, ripping my body from the tendrils of blackness. I landed hard on the stone floor, frozen as I watched the wisps change direction and begin to wrap around Sam. He continued to walk forward and started pulling the blackness from Evie. I reached my hand out toward her as he wrenched the last wisp of darkness from Evie. Our eyes met and then she faded away.

"Evie!" I shouted.

Sam turned to face me, his face covered in tears. "Go now. Thank you," he said.

"Sam! No!" I started to move toward him, but gentle hands pulled me back and turned me away from Sam. I looked up into the quiet countenance of the man in white.

It is his choice, his gift. Don't waste it.

I turned to look back at Sam. His mouth was drawn back in a silent scream, the tendrils of darkness shooting down into his mouth as he was completely immersed in the evil. A moment later, he was gone, completely devoured by the darkness.

Go quickly while it is satiated.

I was crying too hard to fasten my harness completely. The man snapped the buckle shut and reached up to yank twice on the rope.

We will meet again.

I sobbed as Tristan and Andy pulled me up through the well. When I got to the top, I fell into Andy's arms. Every part of me hurt and I wanted to forget everything I saw down there.

Tristan unhooked the rope and shoved the equipment into the backpack.

Andy held me while I cried and they moved me toward the holding cell. Before we went through, he looked at me, his brow furrowed. "Evie?"

I shook my head, a new crop of tears pouring from my eyes.

"Sam?"

My sobs were his answer and we crawled through the hole. We slid our way across the small space and then wiggled into the tiny tunnel. This time, Tristan went first. He stopped several times to look back at me, his headlamp nearly blinding me in the tight quarters. Andy pushed from behind when I faltered. Finally, we came out of the tunnel and stood in the cavern.

"What happened down there?" Tristan asked.

I started to tell him, but then a sound reached my ears. I turned with horror to the hole we came through.

Something was coming. A slick, oily sound reached my ears and I turned to the boys. "We have to go. *Now!*"

We practically ran through the cave, stopping to find the arrows made of reflective tape that Andy placed on our way in. The sound followed us the entire way, so close at times that I thought I would see it grabbing at my heels if I looked down. We finally reached the large cavern on our property and grabbed our coats. Tristan wrapped mine around my shoulders as we ran out the small opening into the snow, Andy and Tristan but steps behind. We stood on the bank of the creek, catching our breath.

Marissssaaaa.

The hissing voice called to me from the yawning opening. I took off, running through the woods toward the house, Andy and Tristan crashing through the underbrush behind me. We didn't stop until we reached Andy's truck.

At that moment, all of our phones began beeping with messages and missed calls. I pulled mine from my coat pocket and swiped the screen.

It was my dad. He'd messaged twenty-six times. They got more and more desperate as I scrolled through.

You should get here soon.

Marissa, things aren't going well.

The doctor says Genevieve isn't going to make it through the night.

She's going soon.

I looked up at Andy and Tristan. Their colorless faces told me that they'd received the same texts. "We have to go to the hospital."

Shaking off our wet, muddy jackets, we threw them in the back of the truck and climbed into the cab. Andy fired it up and peeled out of the driveway. I texted my dad that we were on our way.

He texted back one word: *Hurry.*

CHAPTER 25

Andy squealed into the parking lot of the hospital on two wheels and we jumped out of the truck as soon as it stopped. We rushed through the lobby and into the elevator. I tapped my finger nervously on the button. The noise amplified in the small space. *She'll be there, right? Sam saved her. He sacrificed himself to save her. Now he's gone. She can't be gone, too.* I shook my head to clear it from thoughts of Evie not making it. She had to make it.

I whipped open the door when we got to her room and was met with the sight of my dad, leaned over in a chair, his head resting in his hands. He looked up as we entered, his face gray and his eyes watery. He blinked and his chin trembled when he saw me. He got up and wrapped me in a hug, his breathing uneven with emotion.

"She's going to come back to us," I said, my voice muffled against his chest.

My dad leaned down and kissed the top of my head. "I don't think so, Peanut. I don't think there's much hope now."

I realized that the room was completely quiet. The ever-present whooshing sound of the breathing machine was absent. I pushed away from my dad. "Why is the breathing machine off?"

Dad blinked back tears. "The doctor said that keeping her on the ventilator was no longer a viable option."

The words spun around me. I pushed past him into the room and stood looking at Evie's sleeping face. I leaned down over her. "Genevieve Victoria Patton, you listen to me. I don't know where you are, but you have to get back into your body. You *have* to." My voice cracked as I said those words and tears welled up in my eyes for the third time that night. I looked over at Andy and Tristan who stood in the doorway, looking as helpless as I felt. "I don't understand. Sam sacrificed himself to save Evie! She's supposed to be here!" Anger took over and I drove my fingernails into my palms. "Where is she?" Hot tears spilled forth and I sat down hard in the chair on the other side of her bed. "Where is she?" I reached out to hold Evie's hand. It was cold.

"I'm here, St. Louis."

My head whipped up and I saw Evie standing at the foot of the bed. She looked ragged and pale, like a ghost, and her black curls hung in limp ringlets around her face. There was no life left in her eyes and the sight made my heart ache. I opened my mouth to say something, but she held up a hand.

"I don't want them to know I'm here."

Why not?

"It's going to be easier for them to say goodbye. They've already lost me, St. Louis. You're the only one hanging on."

What are you talking about? This is it! The veil is thin, like Sam said it would be.

Evie grabbed the bed railing and doubled over as if she'd been punched in the stomach. A wail erupted from her mouth, spreading into the room and filling it with sadness. My dad reached up and rubbed his upper arms with his hands, warming them. Tristan leaned into Andy and Andy put a comforting arm around his shoulders.

I'm so sorry, Evie. I am. About Sam. About everything. But you have to get back into your body.

She looked up at me with baleful eyes. "Wish I could. The veil isn't thin enough. I can't get through." She looked down at her body. "It didn't work. It's all for nothing, and now Sam's gone, too."

Evie, you have to try! Don't give up! My breath came hard and fast.

"It's no use, St. Louis. I can't get through."

Something nagged at me. A wisp of a thought that danced around the periphery of my consciousness. I took a centering breath and caught it by its tail before it could slip through again. And, then, there it was. An idea that I knew would work with such crystalline clarity that I almost jumped up out of my chair.

Evie, listen to me. I have one foot in the living world and one in the other world, where you are. What if I bridge the gap between the two worlds? What if you use me to cross over into your body again?

She furrowed her brow. "How?"

I hold your hands. One here, I motioned to the hand holding hers on the bed and held out my other hand to her, *and one here.*

She shook her head. "You know what happens when you touch me."

It's okay, Evie, we have to try.

She shook her head again. "You don't know if it will work."

Well, I know what won't work. Come on. We have to try.

She looked uncertainly out the window for a moment, pressing her lips together. "What the heck, St. Louis, I'll give it a try for you."

And, for Sam.

She smiled, her eyes still filled with sadness and she reached out to take my hand. I felt electricity spread through my fingers as they clamped down on hers. My body went rigid and my head rolled down to my chest as I heard the heart monitor flat line. The long monotonous beep followed me as I jumped back from my body. I watched as Evie's ghost turned into wisps of bright colors and muted colors and dark colors. The tendrils went into my hand, working their way up into my arm and then into my chest, starting down my other arm.

I watched as my dad jumped up and ran to the door shouting for a nurse. Andy and Tristan walked over to me and Andy placed his hand on my shoulder. "Wake up, Anderson, she's gone."

A wisp of bright yellow reached out of me and spread over his hand for a moment before plunging back into me. I heard him laugh. It sounded wildly out of place in the current situation and Tristan turned a scowl at him.

"I'm sorry," he said, stifling a chuckle. "I felt like Evie was here."

A nurse ran in and pulled the bed railing down. "You need to leave, sir. Take the kids and get them out of the room."

The small room filled with nurses and I watched with horror as one began to walk toward me. Evie's essence was nearly to the wrist of my right hand, siphoning into her body's wrist as I watched, the colors tumbling over each other to spread into her body. The nurse pushed Andy and Tristan out of the way and began to shake my shoulder.

Not yet! Just a few seconds more!

The nurse shook my shoulder once more and then turned to the doctor who walked in. "She's unresponsive."

He walked over and took my pulse while the nurses began to prep Evie for CPR. "She has a DNR," he said over his shoulder. The nurses stepped away from the bed and began unhooking machines and pulling wires and tubes from Evie's still body.

I watched the last bit of Evie pour into her body and I slammed back into mine, my eyes flying open as I gulped in a huge breath.

"Come with me," the nurse said, helping me up from the chair.

"Time of death, eleven thirty-two."

I turned, pulling myself from the nurse's grasp. "No!"

I fell to the floor, sobbing. My dad was there, his strong arms pulling me up to him as I cried against his shirt. He was crying too, his chest rising and falling unevenly with his sobs.

Andy sat in a chair, his face blank as Tristan called his mom on the phone.

My entire world crashed in around me and I couldn't breathe. The movement in the room ceased for a moment and I stared past my dad's shoulder. The sheet had been pulled up over Evie's face. I closed my eyes and buried my face in my dad's shoulder.

"Geez, you'd think someone died or something."

Evie's voice filled the room. I took a deep breath. *She was a ghost. That was better than losing her altogether, right?*

I pushed away from my dad and wiped my eyes. When I looked up, my breath caught in my throat. Evie's body was sitting up on the bed, a handful of nurses staring open-mouthed at her as she looked around the room.

"Evie!" I screamed and broke from my dad to run to her bedside. "You're here! You're really here!"

"Yeah," she sighed. "I'm here, St. Louis, right here."

CHAPTER 26

I pulled into Grant's driveway on New Year's Eve at around eight o'clock. I got the wheelchair out of the trunk and wheeled it around to the passenger side of the car.

"I think this is ridiculous," Evie said as soon as I opened the door.

"Doctor's orders," I quipped, putting the footrests down.

"I don't want to sit in that thing."

I leveled my gaze at her. "It's going to get awfully cold out here in the car."

She sighed and glared at me as she stepped out of the car and sat down in the chair. She placed her feet on the rests and leaned back. "Fine, but I want it noted that I am not happy with this situation."

"Duly noted," I said, closing the door and tossing my purse into her lap.

Grant opened the front door and came out to help me push her into the house. "Hey, Evie, looking good." He leaned over and kissed me. "You, too."

I felt heat rise to my cheeks as I pushed her over the threshold into his living room. "Hi, Marissa," his stepmom said, coming from the kitchen, wiping her hands on a towel. "Evie, good to see you're up and around." She glanced at Grant. "Queso is in the crock pot and popcorn's in the bowls. No drinking, no swearing, no bedrooms. Your dad and I will be home at one." She kissed Grant on the cheek and headed out of the room.

Grant flopped down on the couch. I wheeled Evie next to the television and sat down next to Grant. He placed a warm hand on my leg. "How are you feeling?" he asked Evie.

"Like I've been in a fight."

The back door opened and closed and a car started outside.

"What time are Andy and Tristan coming?" he asked.

"They should be here soon."

"Can you talk for a minute?" he asked me.

I looked over at Evie.

"I'm fine, St. Louis. Me and the furniture."

I handed her the remote and followed Grant into the kitchen.

He turned and pulled me into a huge hug and then leaned down and kissed me. The feeling left my legs and I kissed him back, relishing the way his cologne rose up around me. "I'm glad you're here."

"Me, too," I mumbled, sitting down in the chair he offered me.

He stood, leaning against the counter, staring at me.

"What's up?"

"I'm worried about leaving you."

I brushed it off. "That's stupid. I'm fine."

"I used to think that, you know, before I found out what you do."

I bristled. "What's that supposed to mean?"

"Nothing." He held up his hands. "I worry about you. I'm scared you're going to get into a situation you can't handle."

"Like with Evie at the bridge."

He came over and sat down across from me. "Exactly. Listen, I know I can't tell you not to go on ghost hunts…"

"Because I'm going to go anyway."

He smiled. "I know, but I can tell you that I want you to be careful. I care about you, Marissa. A lot. And, I don't want anything to happen to you."

"I know. I'll be careful."

He sat back and looked at me, his eyes gentle. "I'm really going to miss you."

"You're only going to be a couple hours away."

"I know." He laughed. "I can still miss you, though."

The doorbell rang and Andy and Tristan came in. "Go greet your guests," I teased.

Later that night, I was out on the front porch, my coat wrapped around me as I watched my breath rise up into the cold night air. I was thinking about Kristen, Hannah, and Amalie. I was thinking about Theodore and Mary. And, I was thinking about Sam. I heard the door open behind me and I turned to see Evie sneaking out the front door.

"What are you doing?" I asked.

She jumped about a foot in the air.

"Where's your chair?"

"Andy and Tristan are using it to do wheelies in the kitchen." She made her way slowly over to the front porch swing, the chains rattling as she sat down. "I'm fine, really."

I turned around and leaned back against the porch railing. "How much do you remember about that night?" I asked.

She took a deep breath. "Almost everything. When I went down in the well, I couldn't get away, and the weird thing was, I really didn't want to. It was like everything that had ever meant anything to me was ripped away and all that was left was sadness."

I understood exactly what she meant.

"Do you think Sam is still…around?"

I hesitated, gauging my response. I saw Sam again, his face drawn tight with pain as he was devoured by the darkness. "I'm sorry, Evie. I don't think so."

She sighed.

"I don't think you should try to contact him either."

Evie looked up at me. "I-I…"

"I would want to try it too. I think we should get rid of the Ouija board. I don't think it's safe anymore."

She nodded.

We were quiet for a bit. The icy air bit into my cheeks. It was almost midnight.

"What do you think he meant by *they all stay here?*" Evie asked.

A sonic boom traveled up the street toward me. It scattered dry leaves in its wake as it moved along. I took a step back and put my arm out protectively in front of Evie.

"What is it?"

"I don't know. Something about what you said," I leaned up over the railing as the boom ebbed, moving away down the street away from me. "Something's changed, though."

"Let's go in. I'm getting cold."

"Okay," I said, helping her up from the swing. As we walked toward the door, I heard movement behind me. I turned and saw a man shuffling up the street. Another man walked on the sidewalk across the way. A woman sat on the front porch of the house next to us. She held a glass of iced tea in her hand as she rocked back and forth on the rocking chair. Her hair was pulled into finger rolls and the full skirt of a yellow dress spread out around her saddle shoes. I blinked.

"What's wrong, St. Louis?"

"Hold on." I stepped to the railing and looked out. People were out everywhere, moving along the street and the sidewalks. Pushing lawnmowers through the snow, walking leashes with no dogs, and rolling hoops down the street with sticks. "What is this?" I whispered. I looked in the window of the house across the street. A couple sat at the dining room table playing cards. Another couple, dressed in Victorian clothing danced together in the corner and another woman dressed in a Little House on the Prairie dress rocked a baby in her arms.

Evie came over to stand beside me.

"Do you see this?" I asked.

"See what?"

"All of these people. There are layers and layers of people here. All from different times." I swallowed.

It keeps them here. All of them.

Acknowledgements

Thank you to my husband and daughter who give me the support and love that I need to do this.

Thank you to Amanda Booloodian who allows me to bounce unending ideas off her ears and always comes back with a question to my answers. Thank you to my faithful, amazing beta readers, Roger Bolle and Julie Bolle, who tell it to me straight, even when it's hard.

Thank you to Didi Lawson, who provided translations to German and wrote a beautiful lullaby to include in this book. Thank you to my fantastic editor, Frankie Sutton, for her patience, caring insights, and wonderful attention to detail. Thanks, as well, to Covered Creatively for another amazing cover design and to Vicki Deiter for her formatting expertise.

Ghost Hunters Society Series:

Book One: The Weeping Bridge
Book Two: The Devil Doll
Book Three: The Burning Bride
Book Four: The Widow's Locket
Book Five: The Hoodoo Princess

Other YA books by Adria Waters:

Always Sweet Sixteen
The Edge of Lucidity

ABOUT THE AUTHOR

Adria Waters is the author of the Ghost Hunters Society series and has seen ghosts all her life. She loves exploring the paranormal and goes on ghost tours in every place she visits. When she's not hunting ghosts, she loves taking her family on road trips across the country to see every single sightseeing opportunity in the United States. Adria lives in Missouri with her very patient husband, her not-so-patient daughter, a herd of cats who insist that they are human, and various little spirits that pop up to say "hello" once in a while.

You can find out more about Adria and her writing at
www.AdriaWaters.com

www.ingramcontent.com/pod-product-compliance
Lightning Source LLC
Chambersburg PA
CBHW060402260626
47160CB00006B/2399